Meet
Maud
the Koala

by J. E. Morris

Penguin Workshop

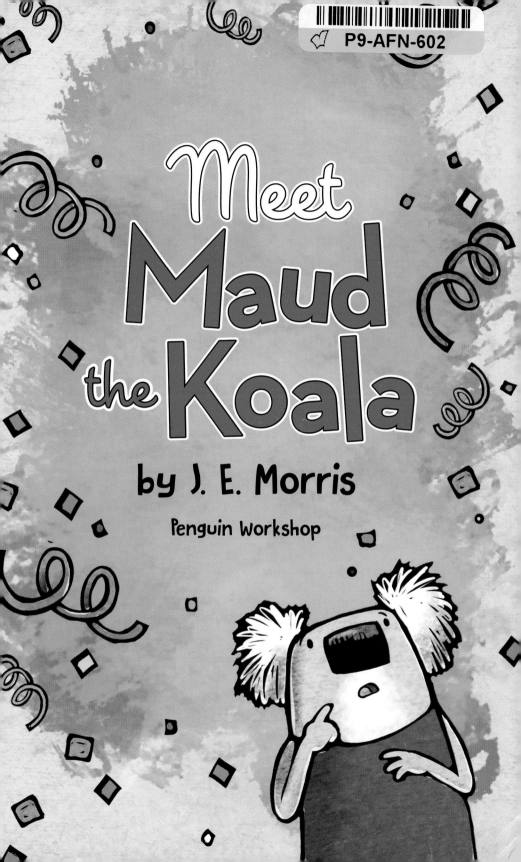

PENGUIN WORKSHOP
An Imprint of Penguin Random House LLC, New York

Copyright © 2018 by Jennifer Morris. All rights reserved. *Fish Are Not Afraid
of Doctors* and *Much Too Much Birthday* first published in 2018 by Penguin Workshop.
This bind-up edition published in 2020 by Penguin Workshop, an imprint of
Penguin Random House LLC, New York. PENGUIN and PENGUIN WORKSHOP
are trademarks of Penguin Books Ltd, and the W colophon is a registered
trademark of Penguin Random House LLC. Manufactured in China.

Visit us online at www.penguinrandomhouse.com.

The Library of Congress has cataloged the individual books under the
following Control Numbers: *Fish Are Not Afraid of Doctors*: 2018004225,
Much Too Much Birthday: 2018004227.

ISBN 9780593094365   10 9 8 7 6 5 4 3 2 1

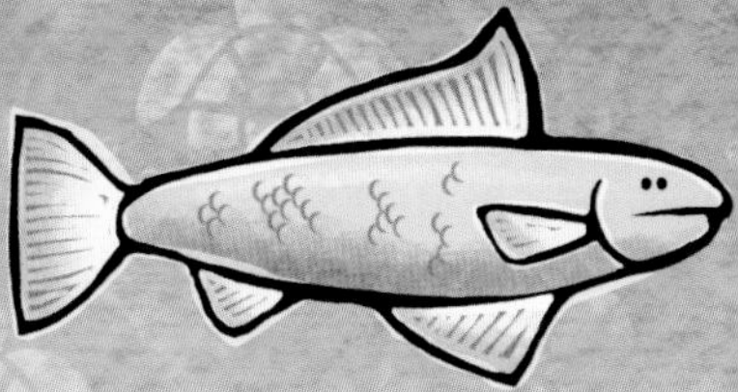

Fish Are Not Afraid of Doctors

by J. E. Morris

To the staff at MGH and healthcare professionals everywhere—thank you!

—JEM

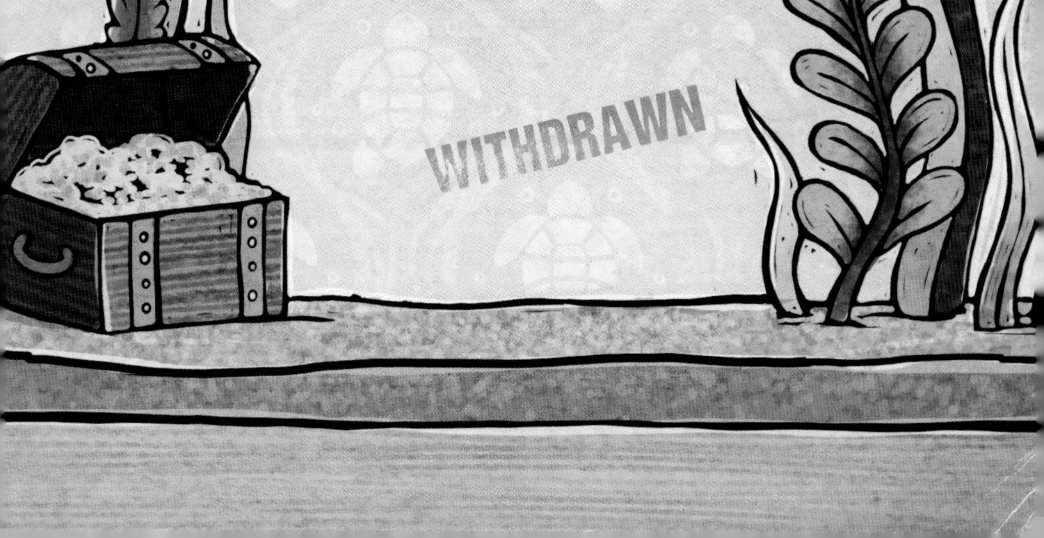

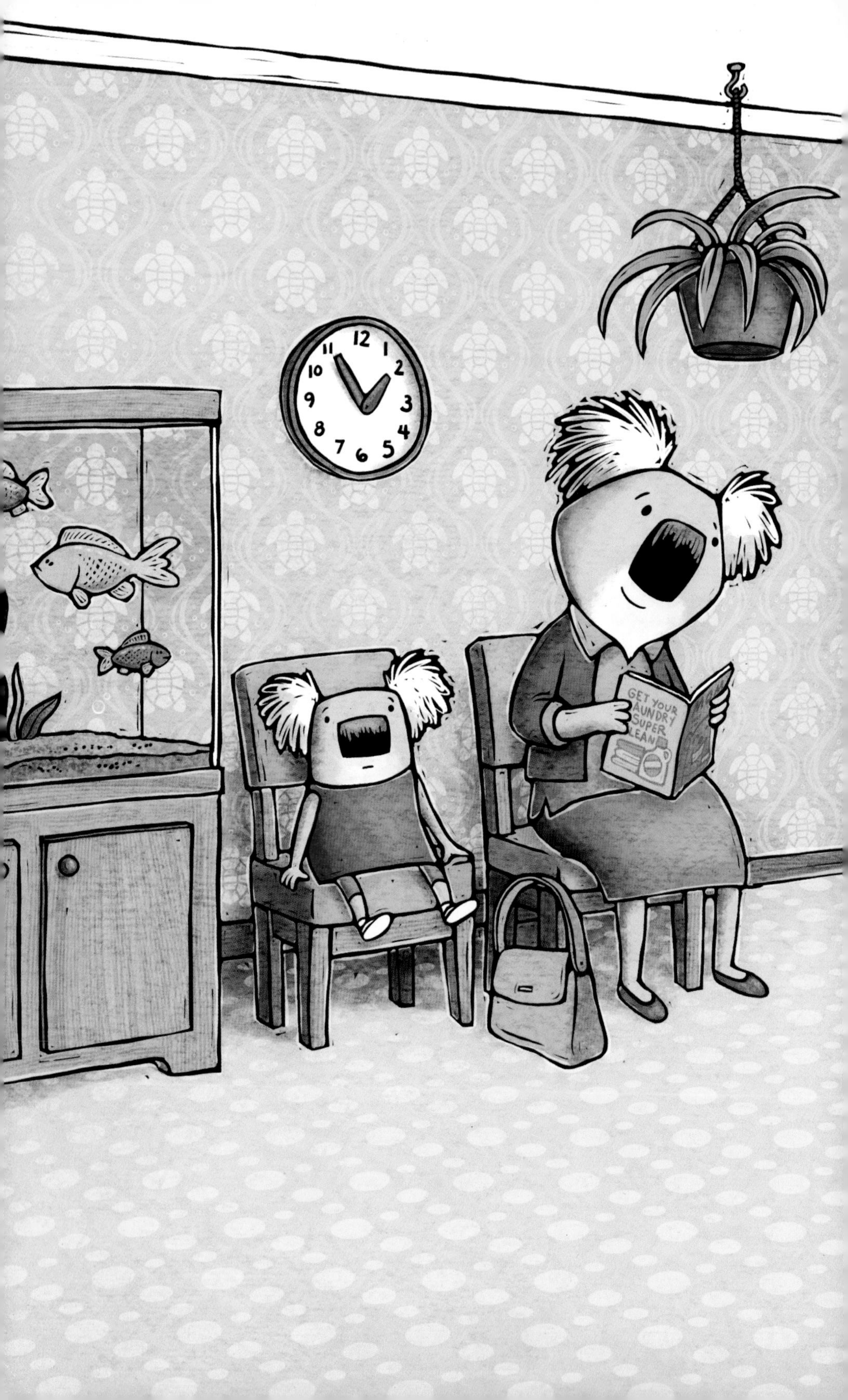
GET YOUR
AUNDRY
SUPER
LEAN

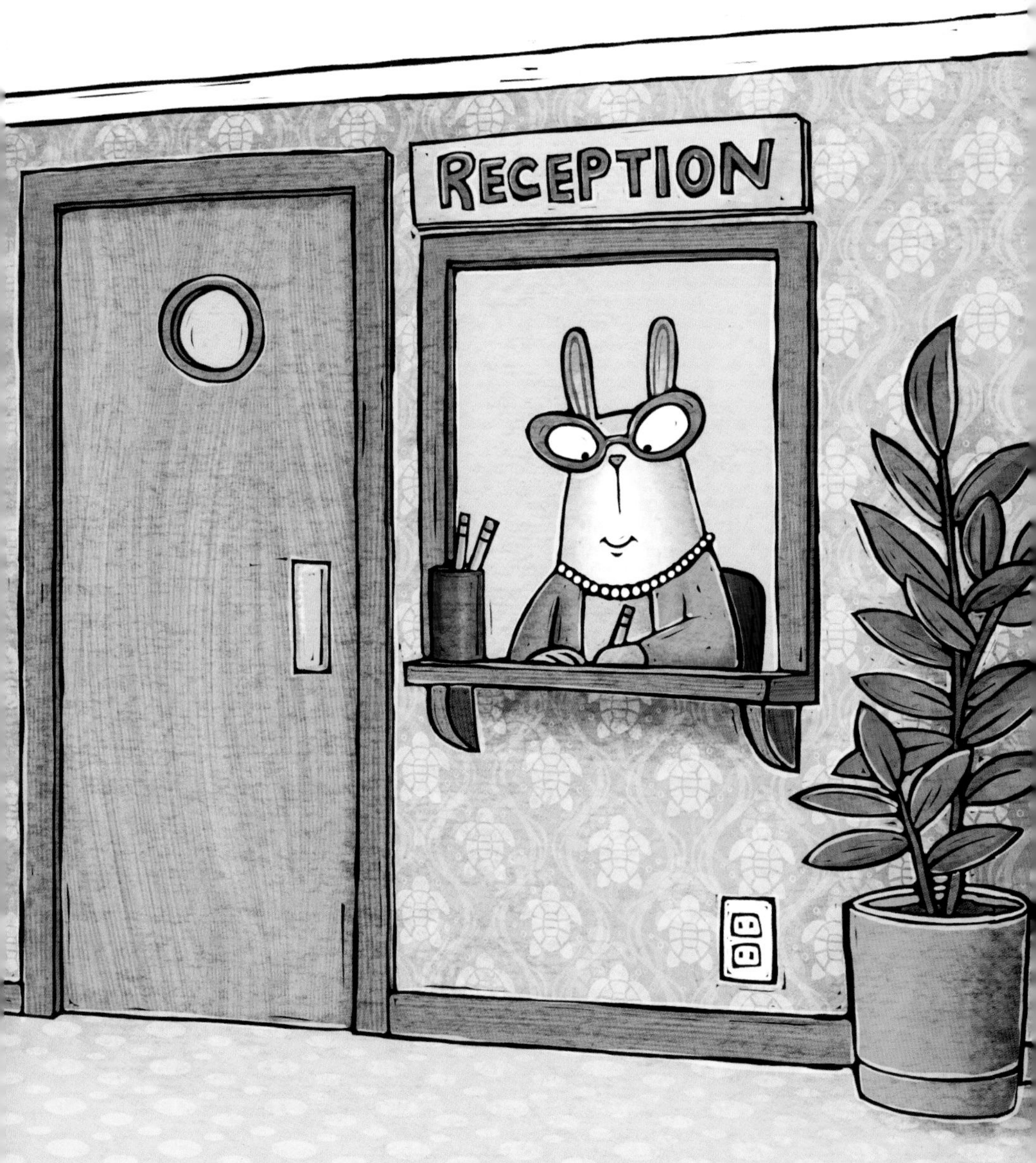
RECEPTION

Maud went to see Doctor Susan
for a checkup.

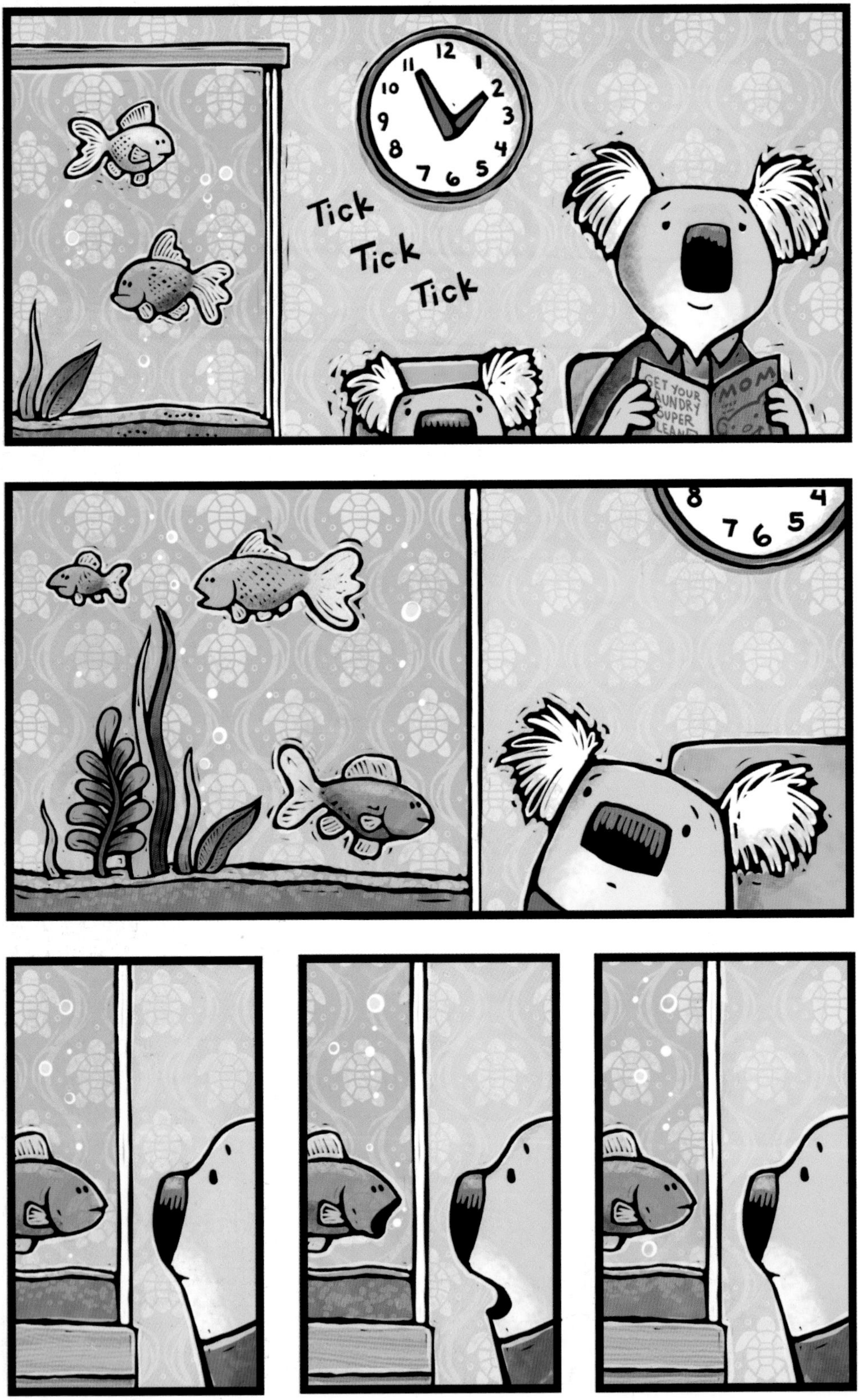
Tick
Tick
Tick
GET YOUR
AUNDRY
UPER
LEAN
MOM

"Do you think fish are afraid of doctors?" asked Maud.

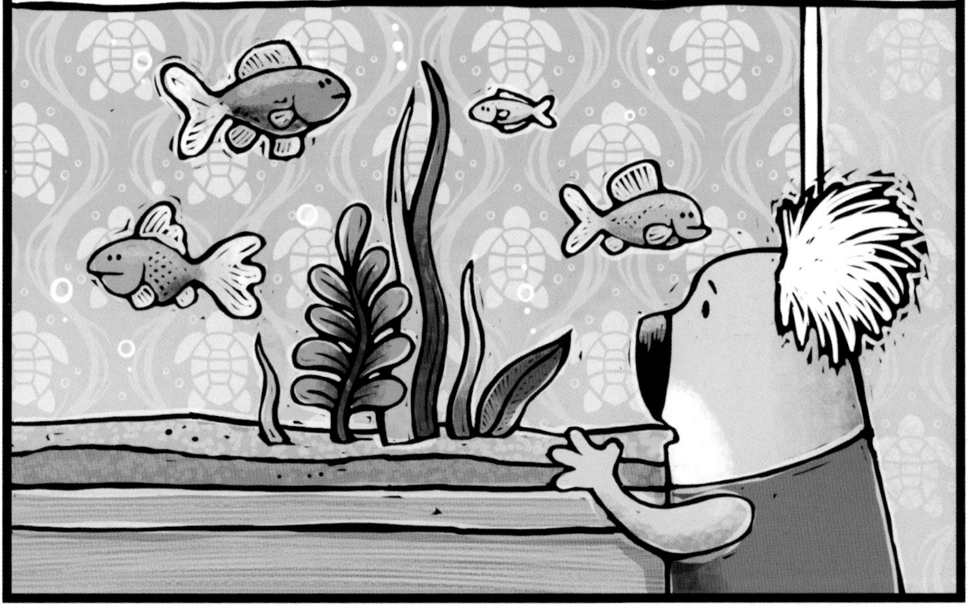

"Fish don't go to the doctor," said Mother.

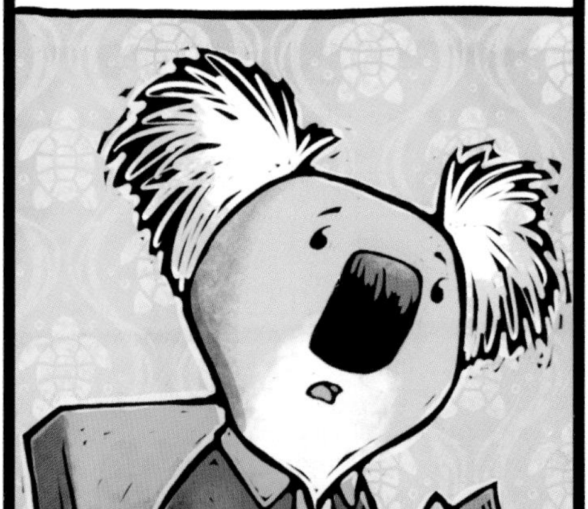
GET YOUR
LAUNDRY
SUPER

"I wish I was a fish," said Maud.

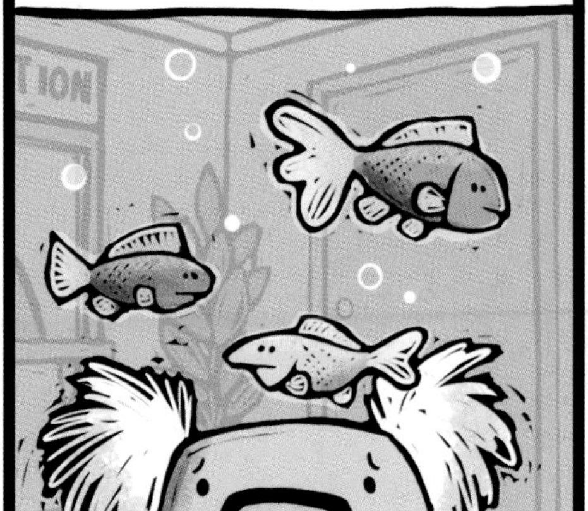

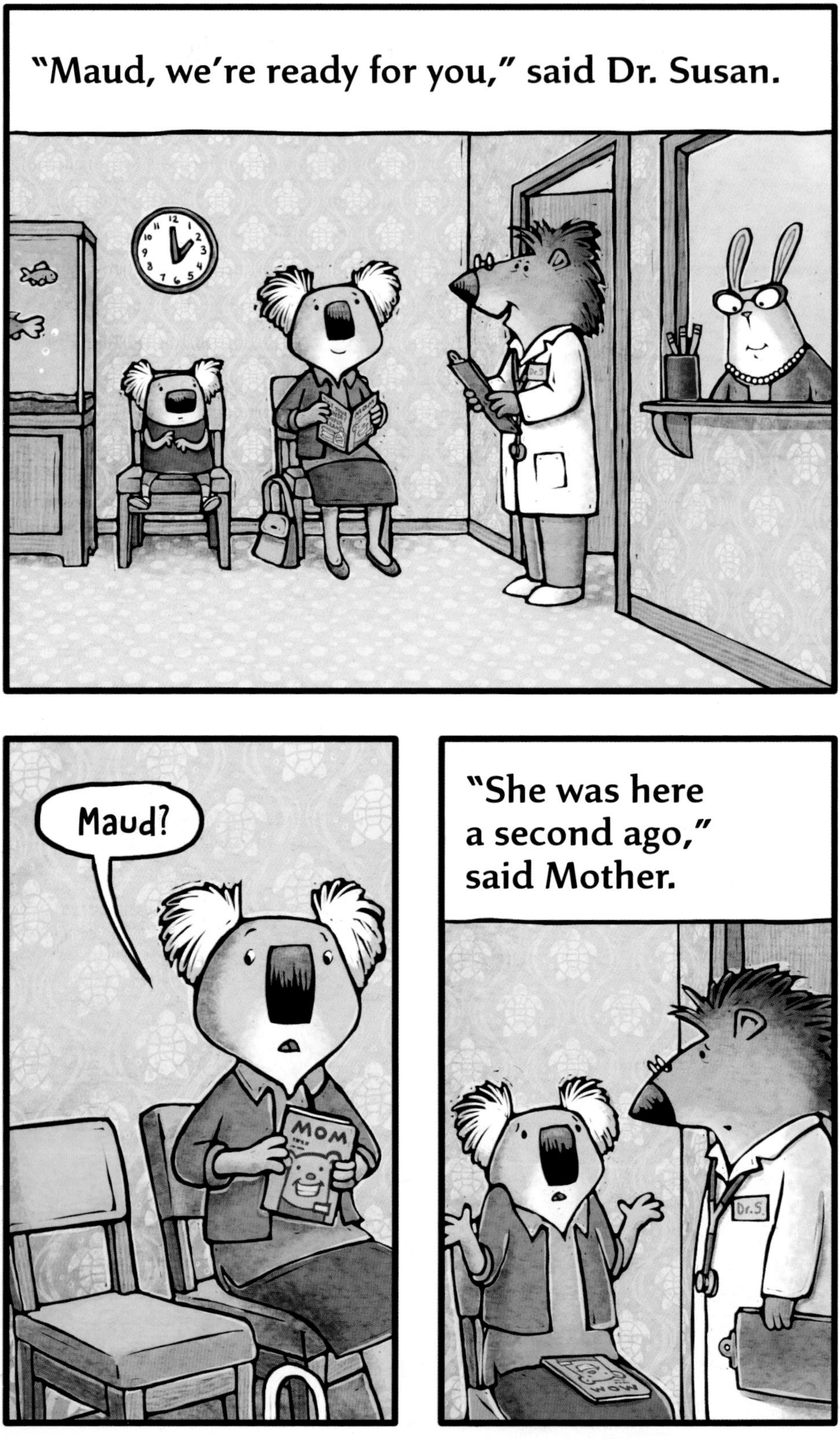
"Maud, we're ready for you," said Dr. Susan.
Maud?
"She was here a second ago," said Mother.

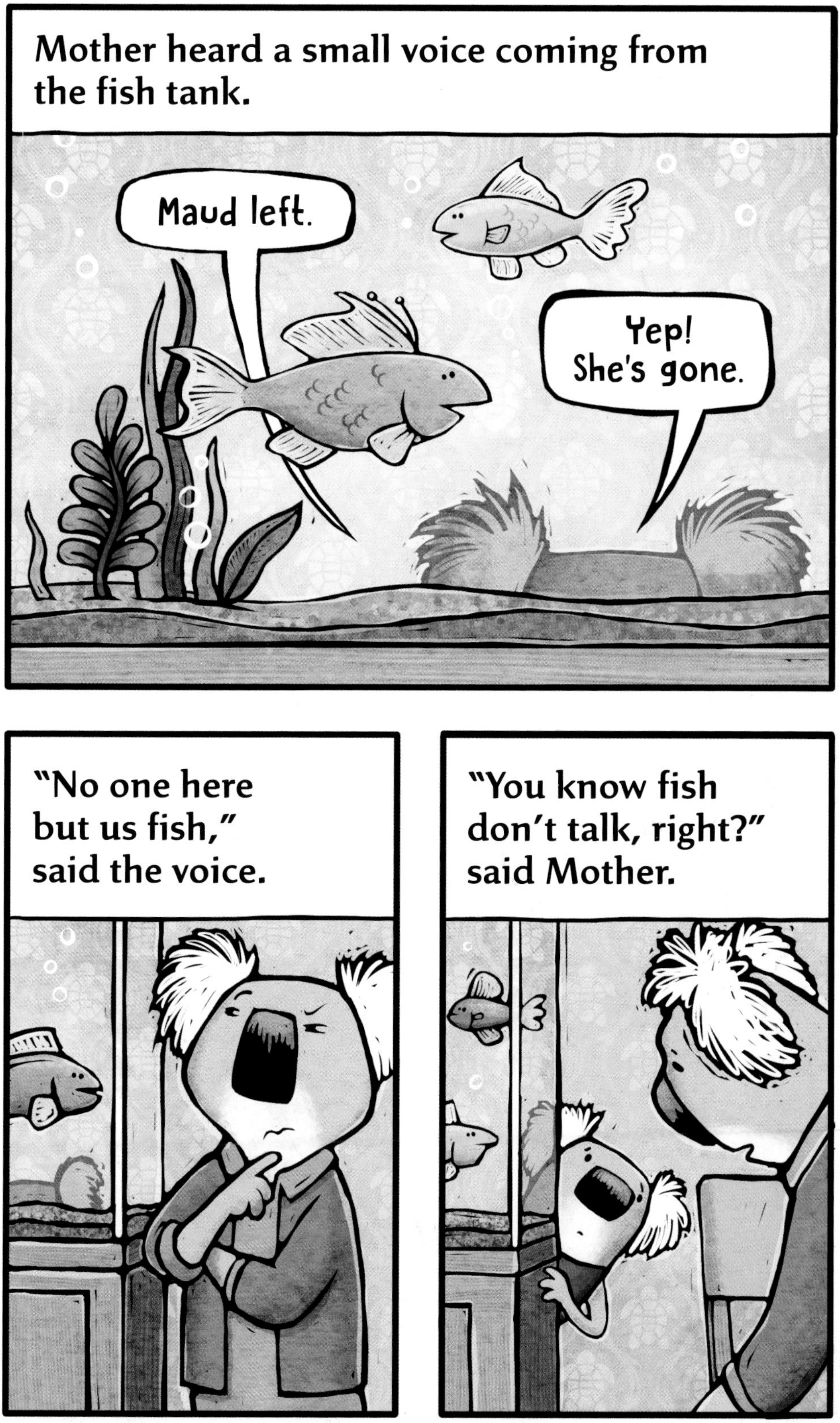
Mother heard a small voice coming from the fish tank.
Maud left.
Yep! She's gone.
"No one here but us fish," said the voice.
"You know fish don't talk, right?" said Mother.

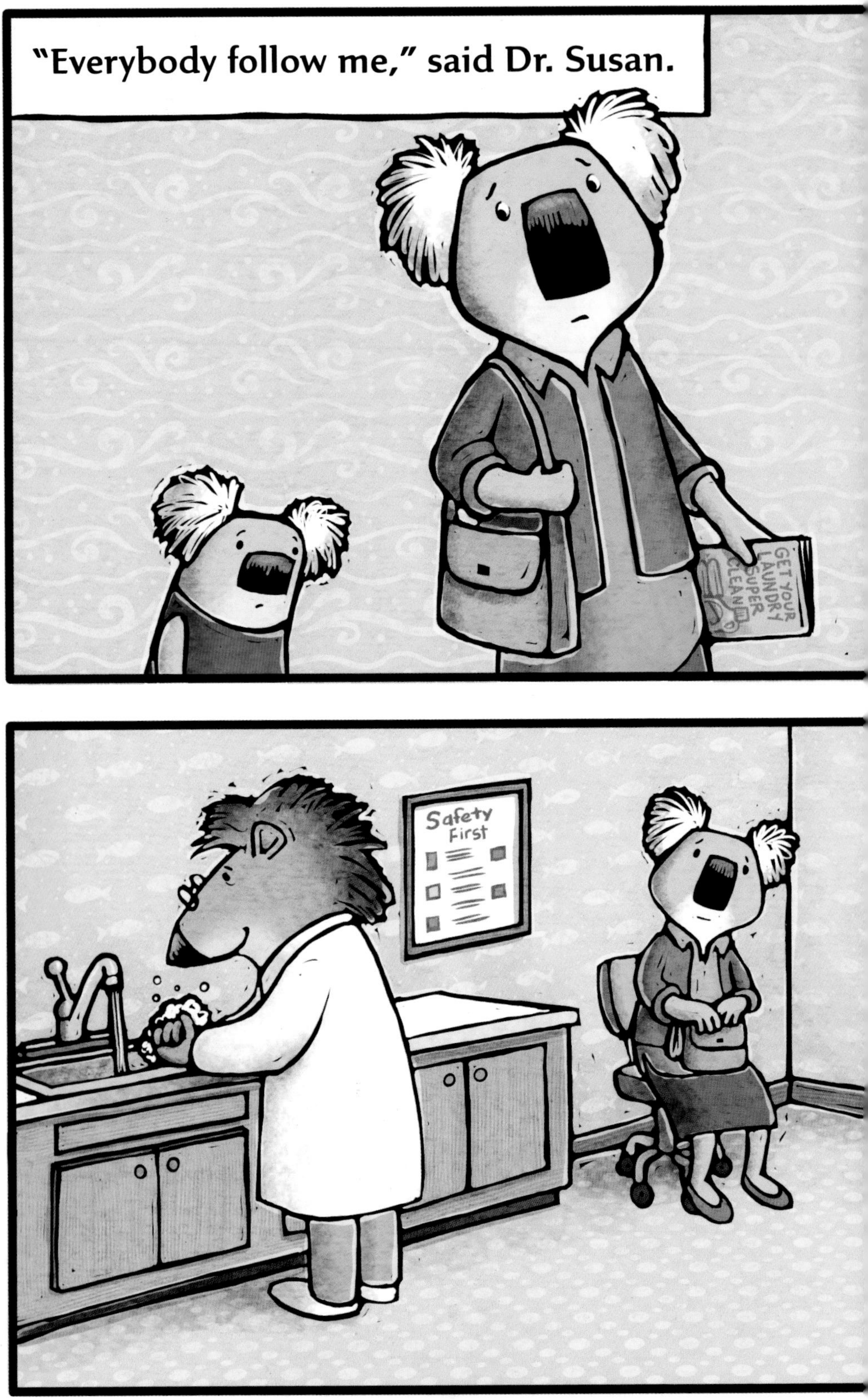
"Everybody follow me," said Dr. Susan.
GET YOUR LAUNDRY SUPER CLEAN
Safety First

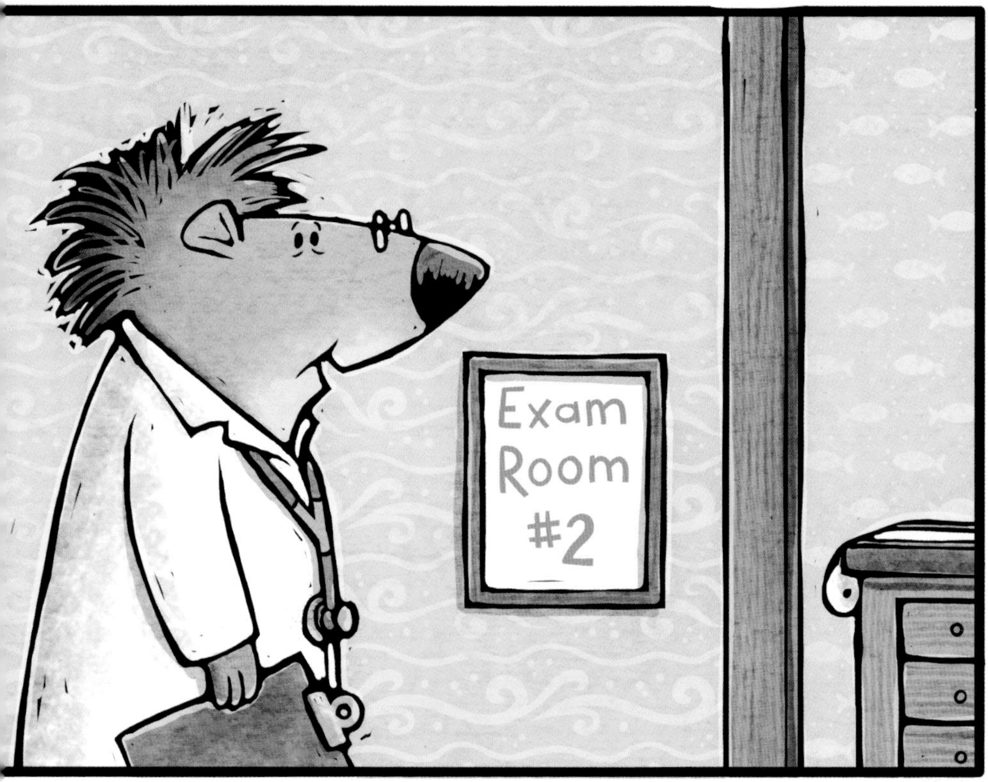
Exam
Room
#2

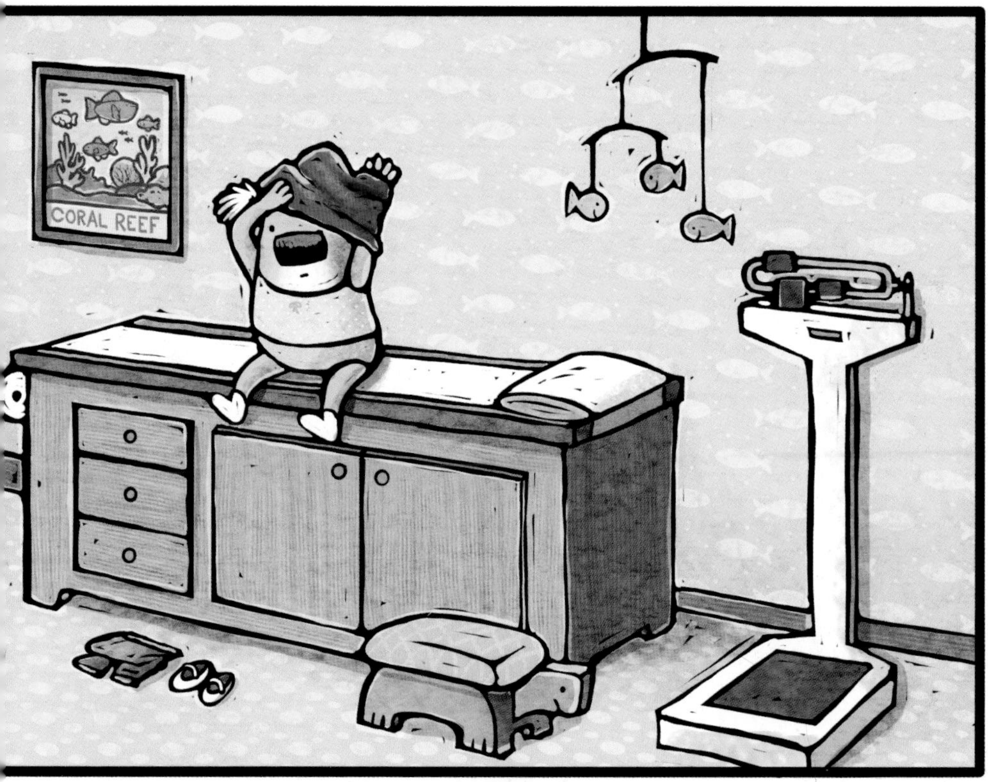
CORAL REEF

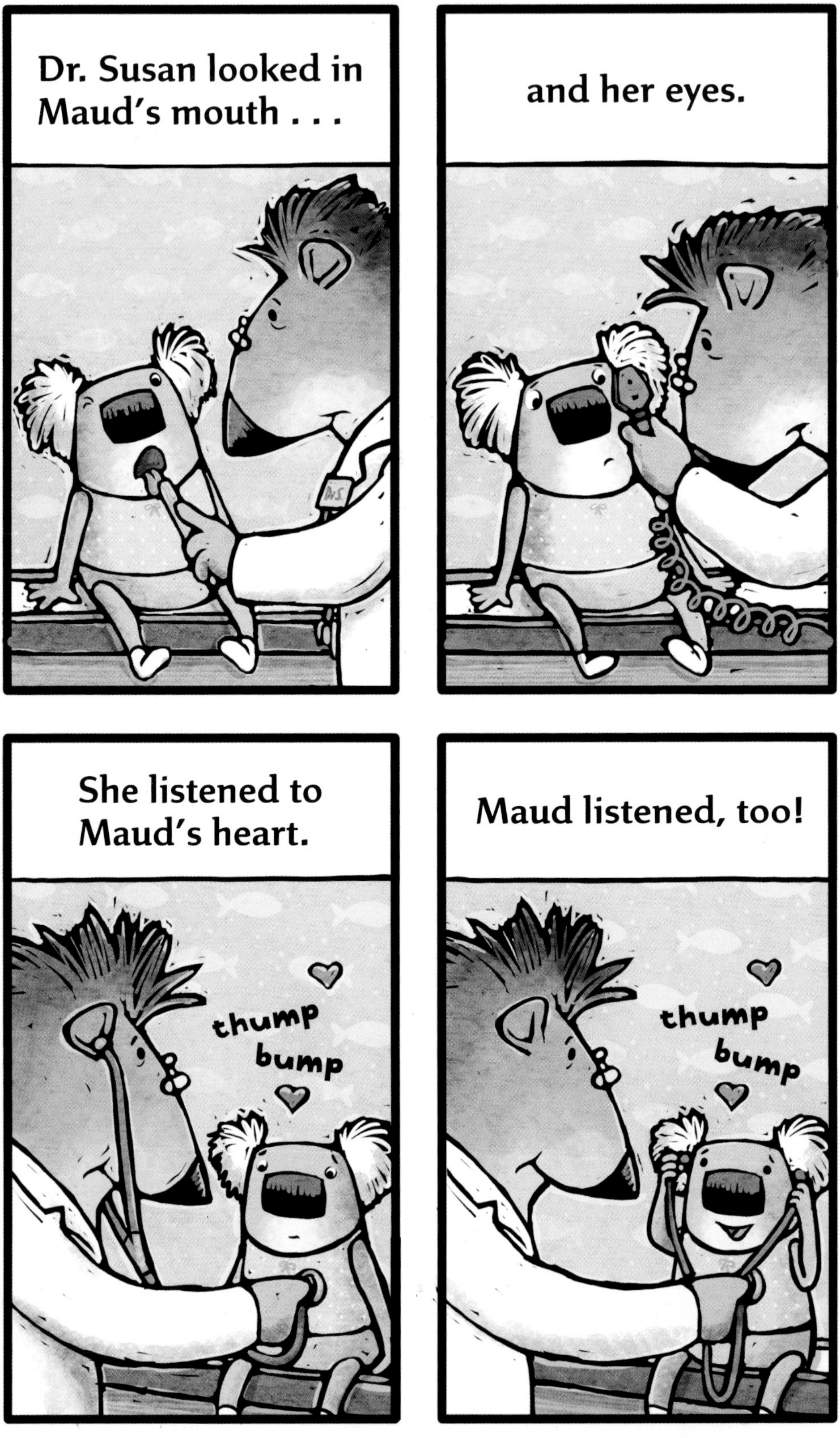
Dr. Susan looked in Maud's mouth . . .
and her eyes.
She listened to Maud's heart.
thump
bump
Maud listened, too!
thump
bump

"Everything looks good," said Dr. Susan. "All you need now is a vaccination."

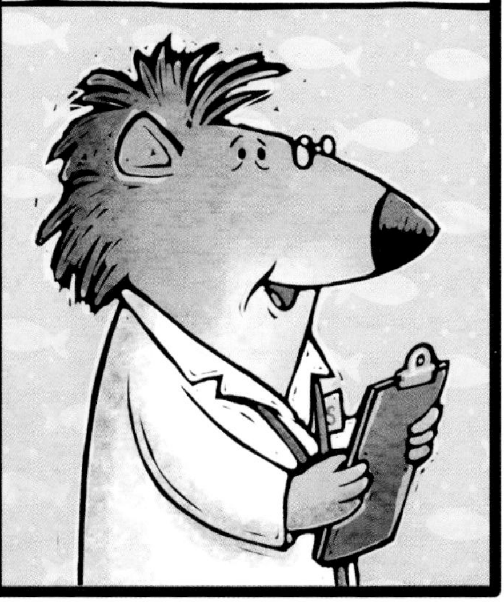

"What's a vax-i-nay-shun?" asked Maud.

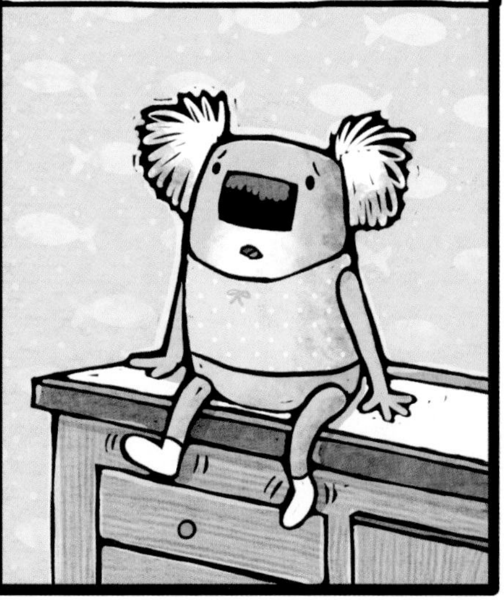

"It's just a teeny tiny little shot. You will hardly feel it," said Dr. Susan.

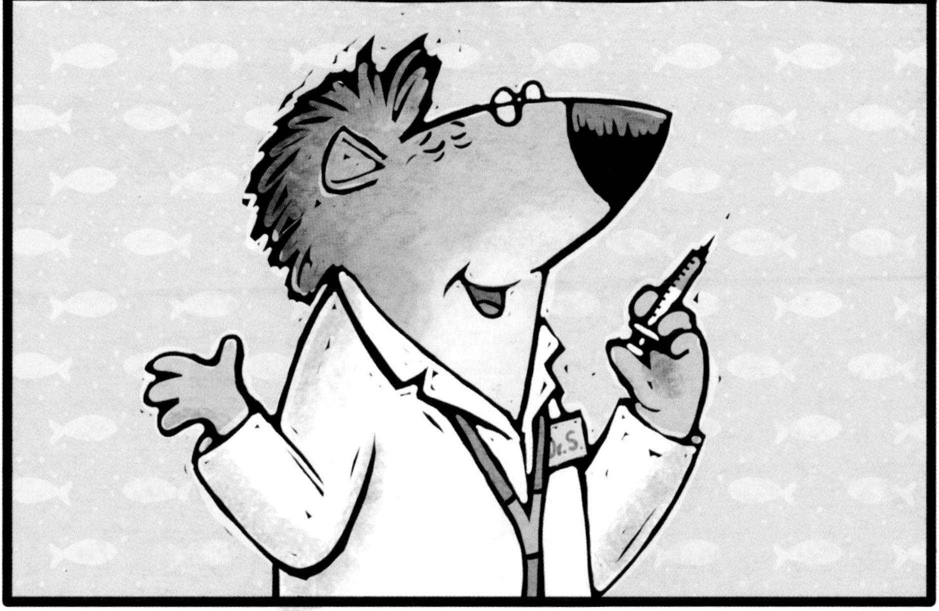
Dr.S.

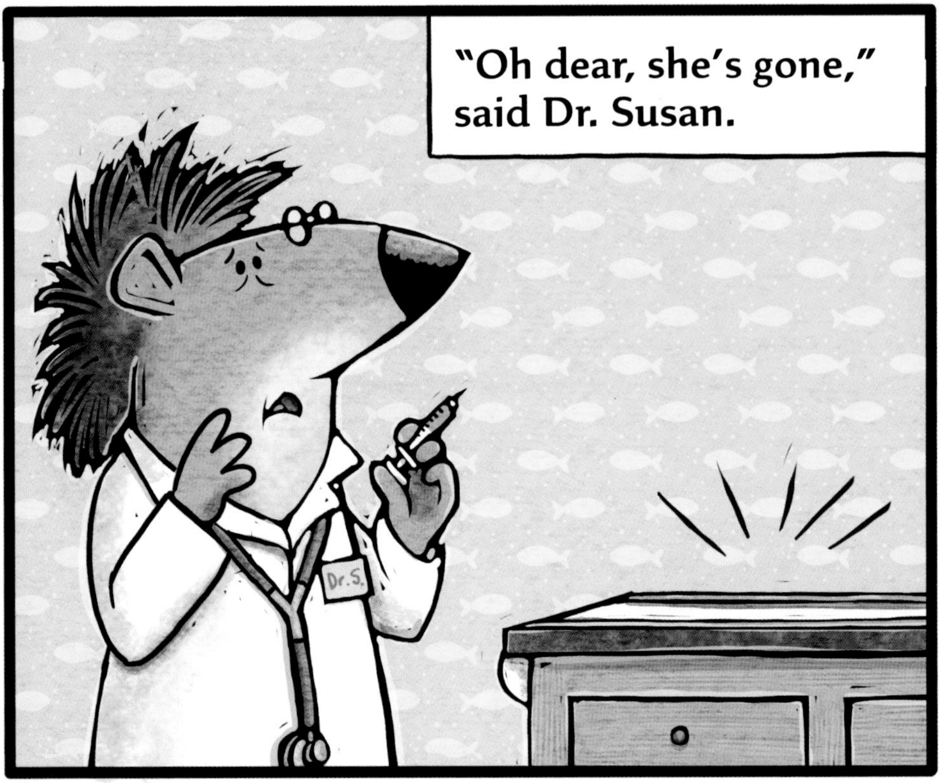
"Oh dear, she's gone," said Dr. Susan.
Dr. S.

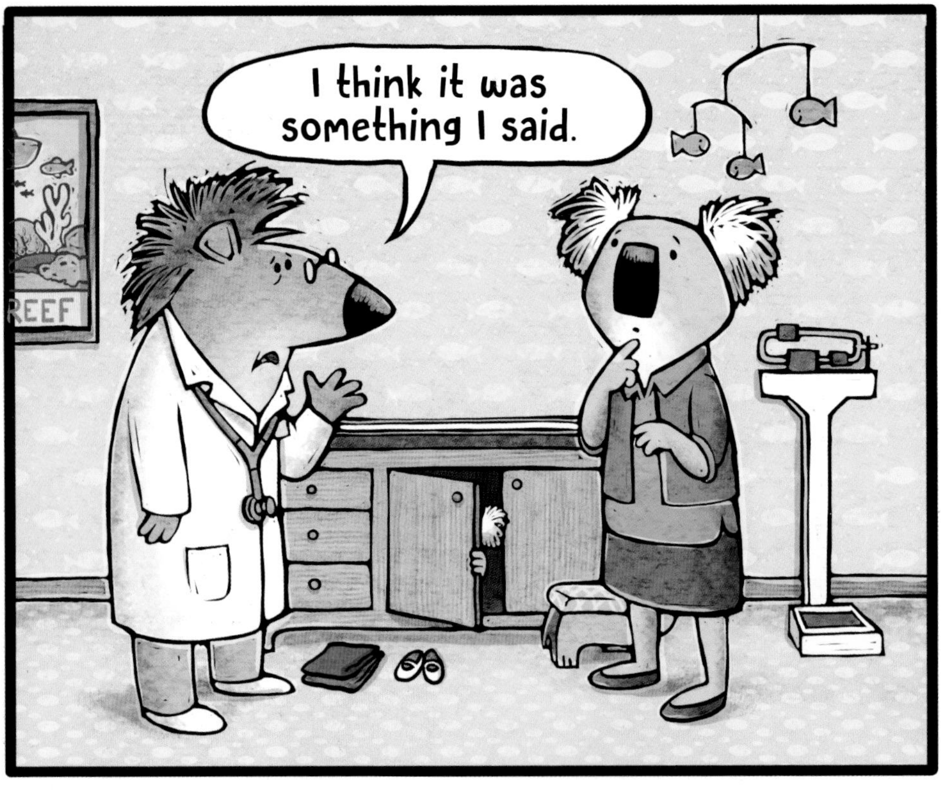
I think it was something I said.
REEF

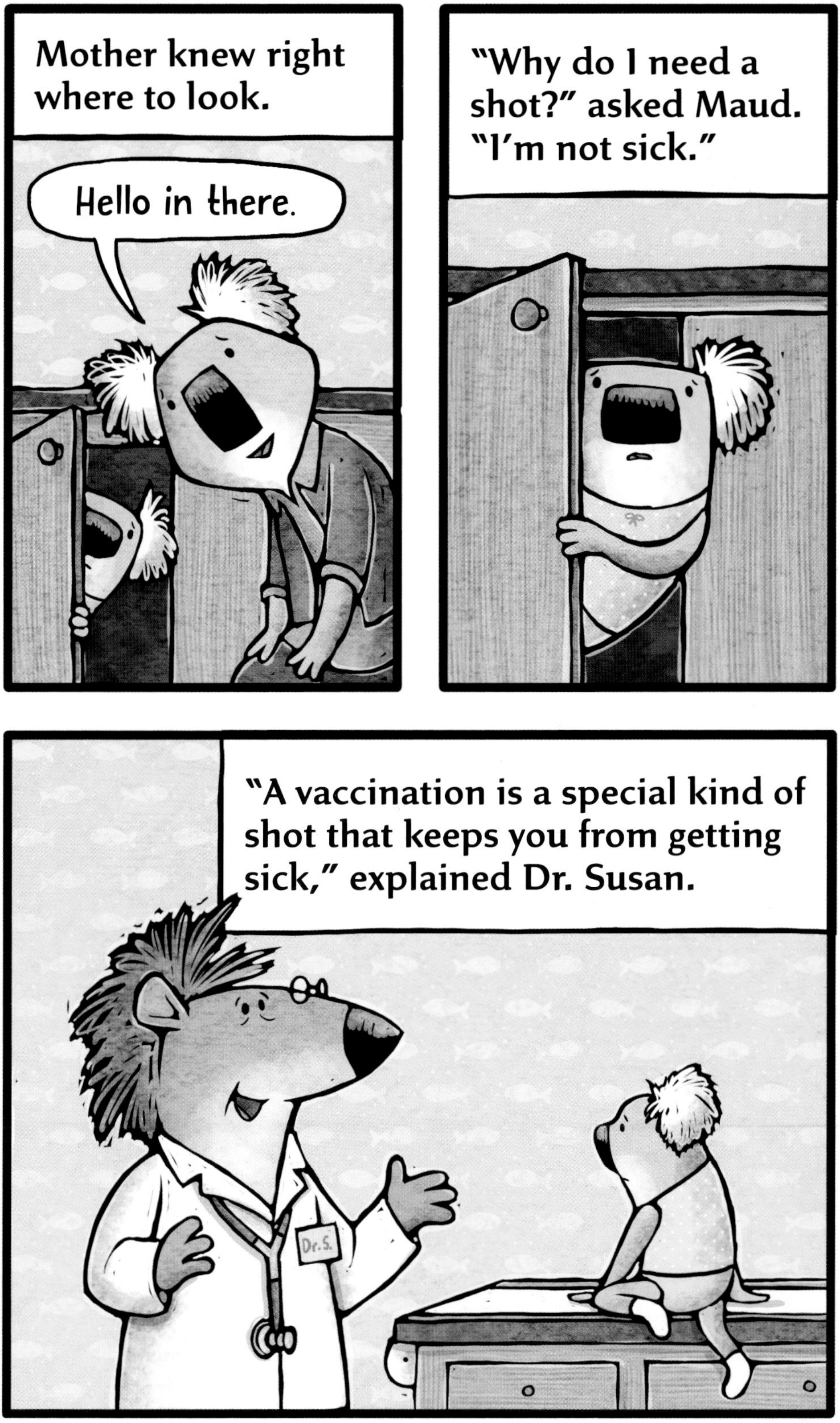
Mother knew right where to look.
Hello in there.
"Why do I need a shot?" asked Maud. "I'm not sick."
"A vaccination is a special kind of shot that keeps you from getting sick," explained Dr. Susan.

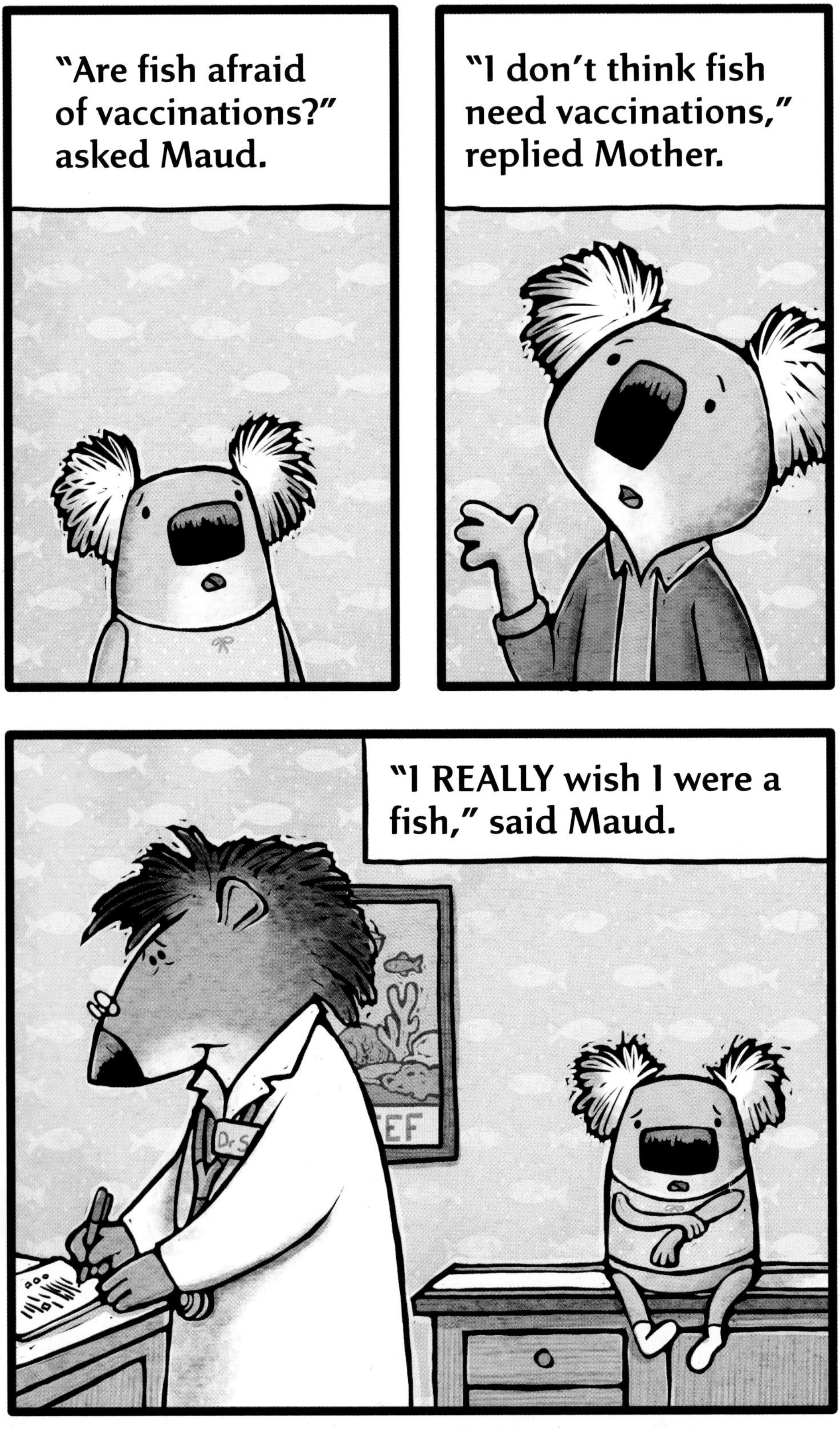
"Are fish afraid of vaccinations?" asked Maud.
"I don't think fish need vaccinations," replied Mother.
"I REALLY wish I were a fish," said Maud.

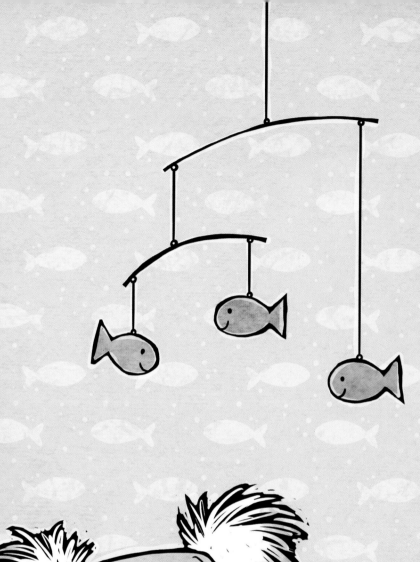

Sigh

Maud shut her eyes.

She pretended that she had two floppy fins!

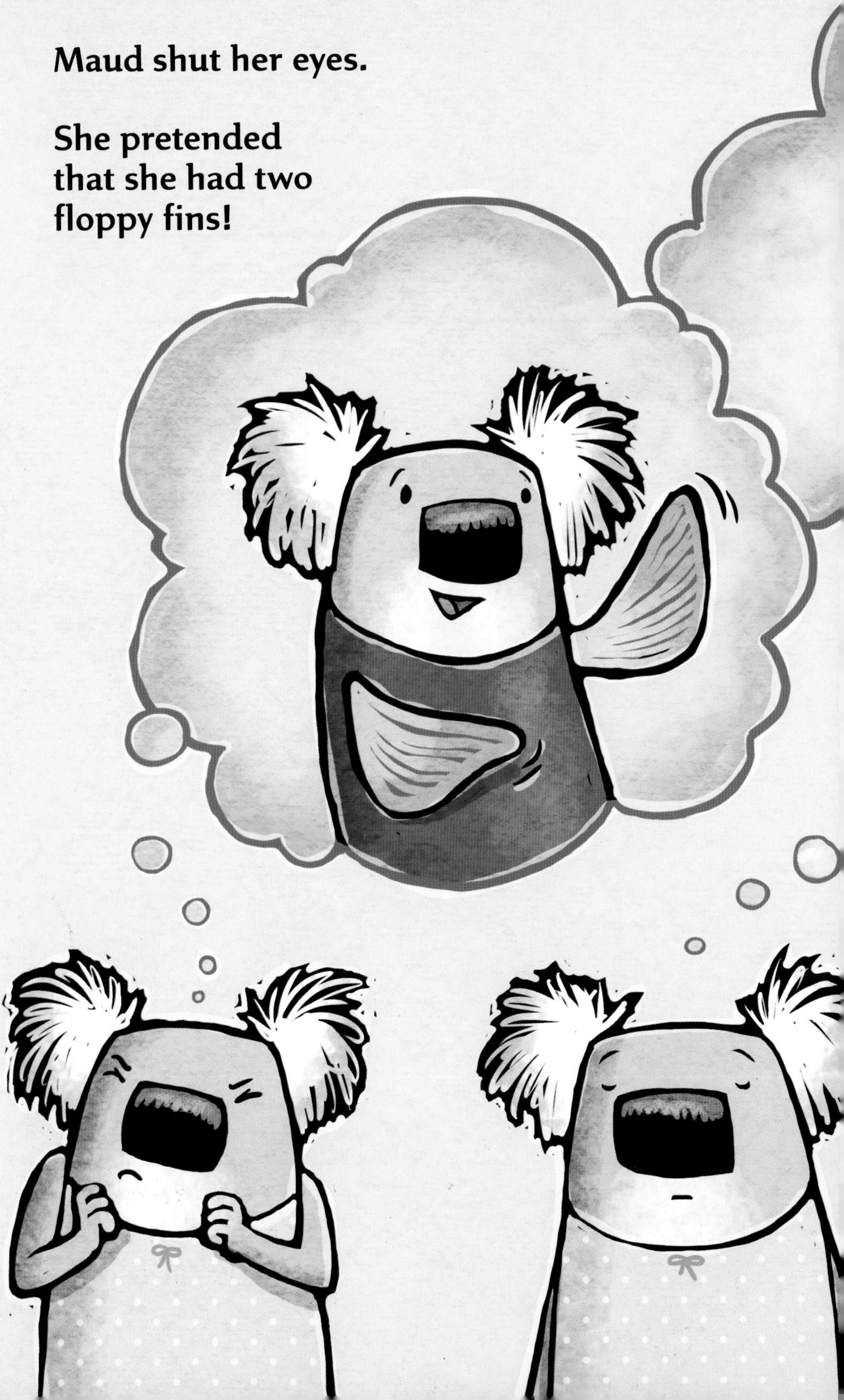

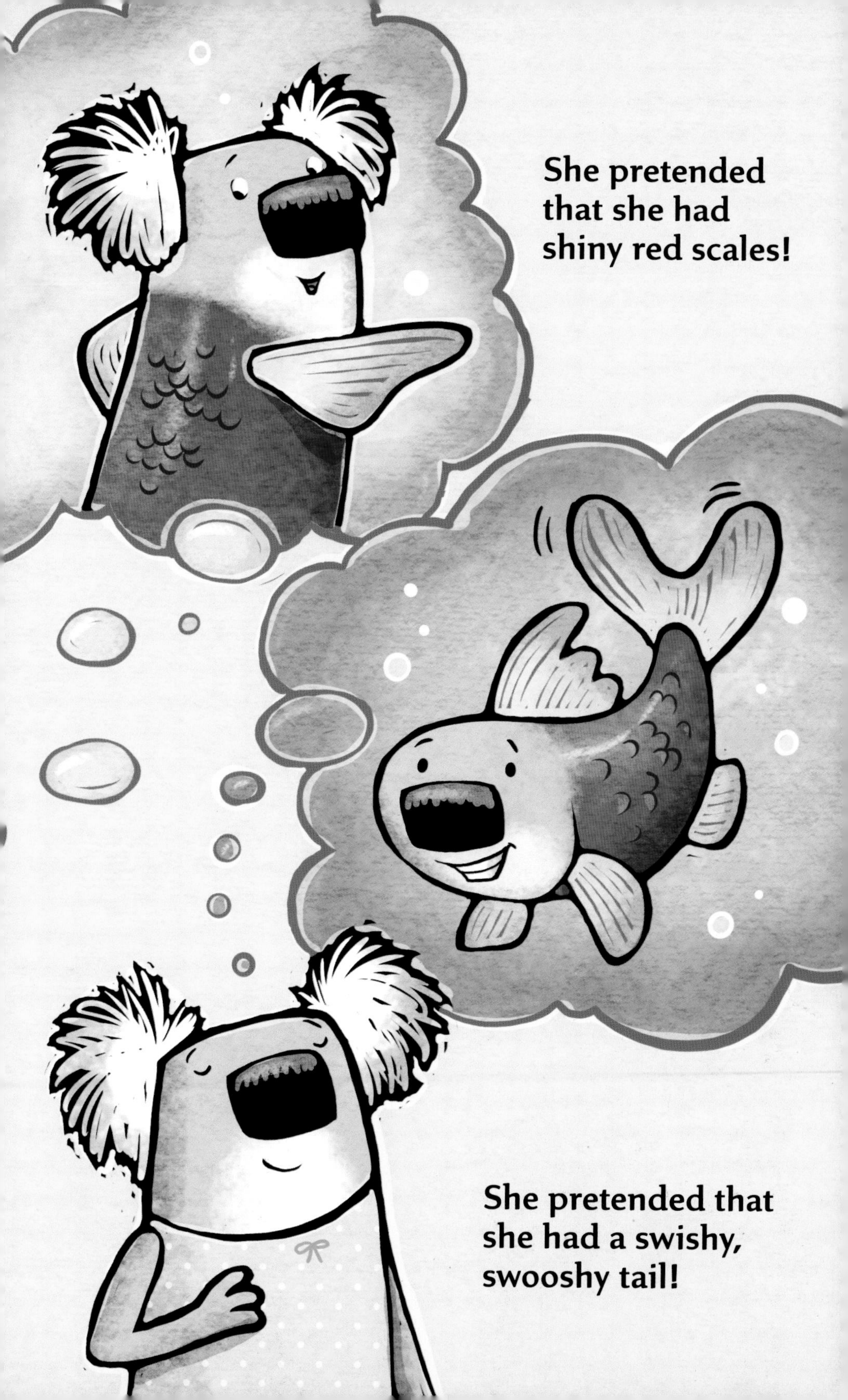

She pretended that she had shiny red scales!

She pretended that she had a swishy, swooshy tail!

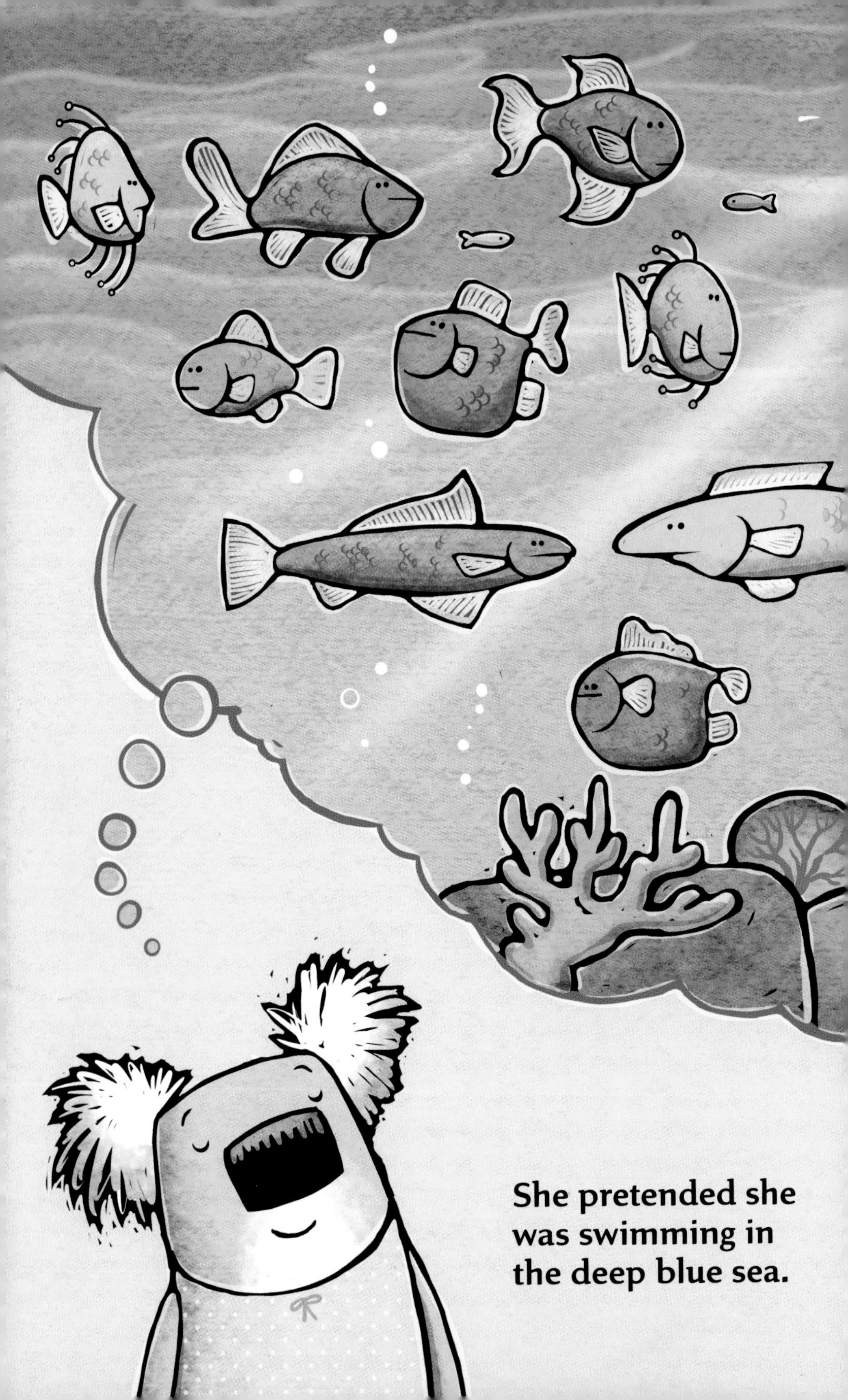

She pretended she
was swimming in
the deep blue sea.

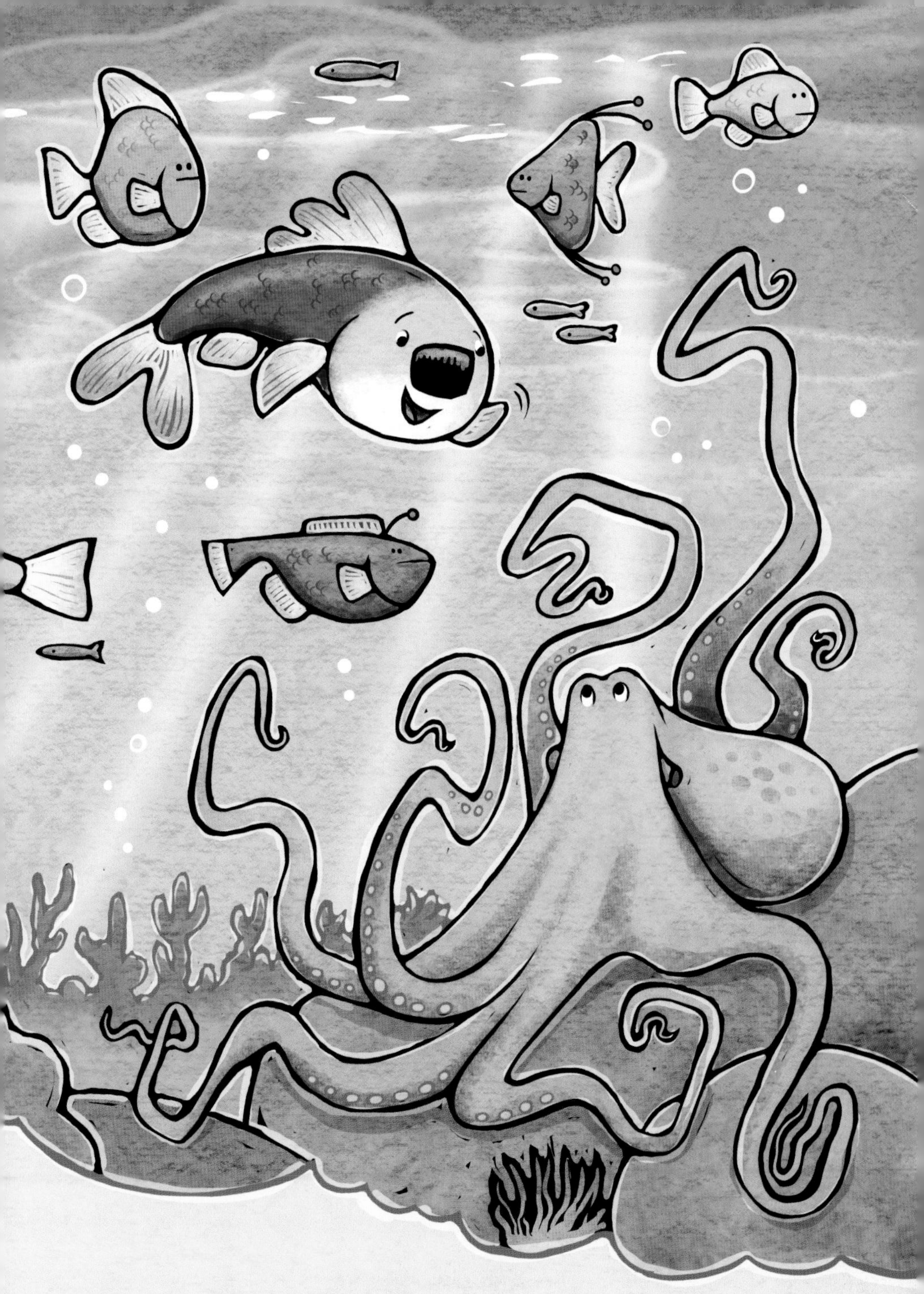

She saw lots of colorful fish.
She even saw a big squiggly octopus.

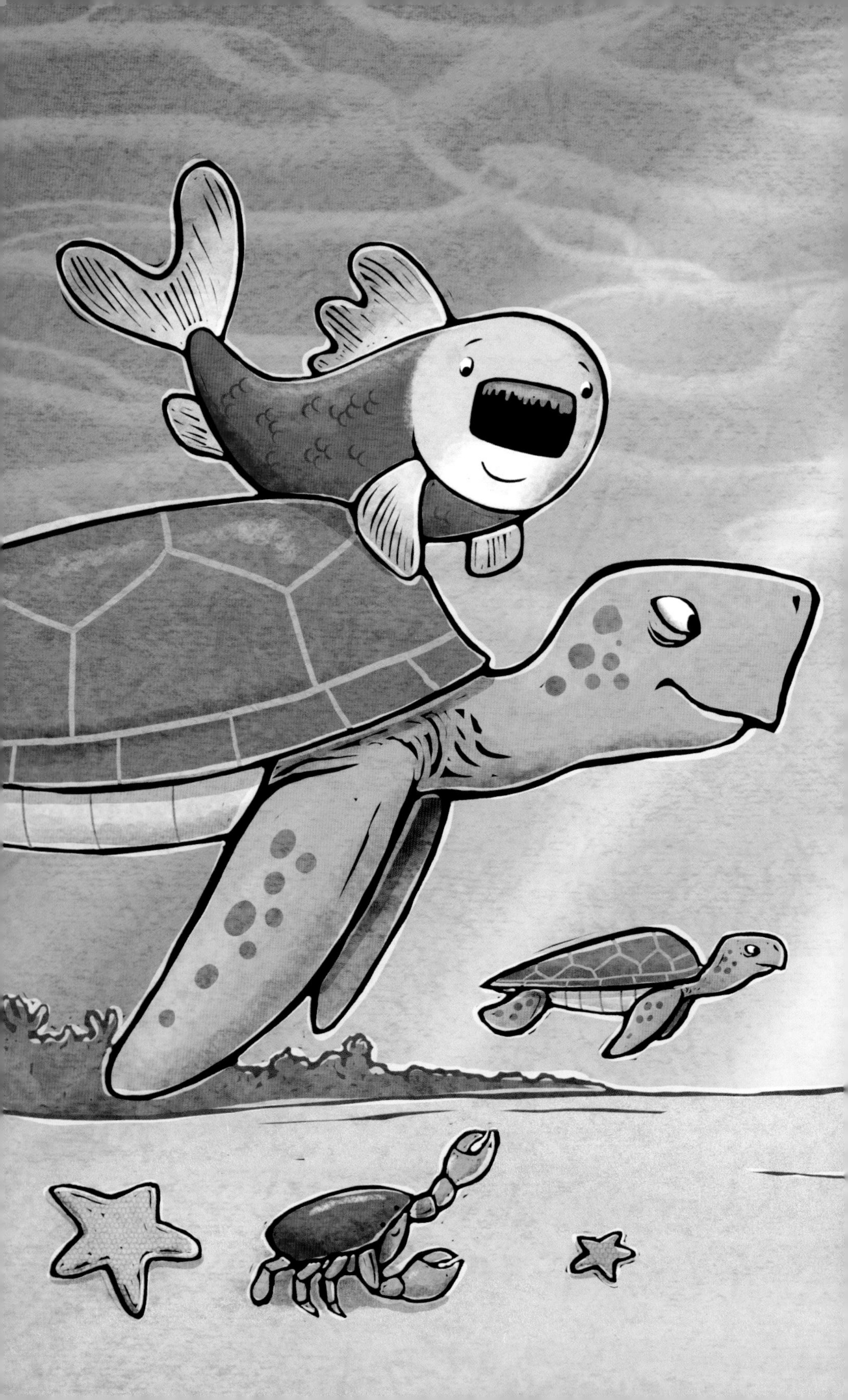

She found a herd of sea turtles.
She patted their smooth, hard shells.

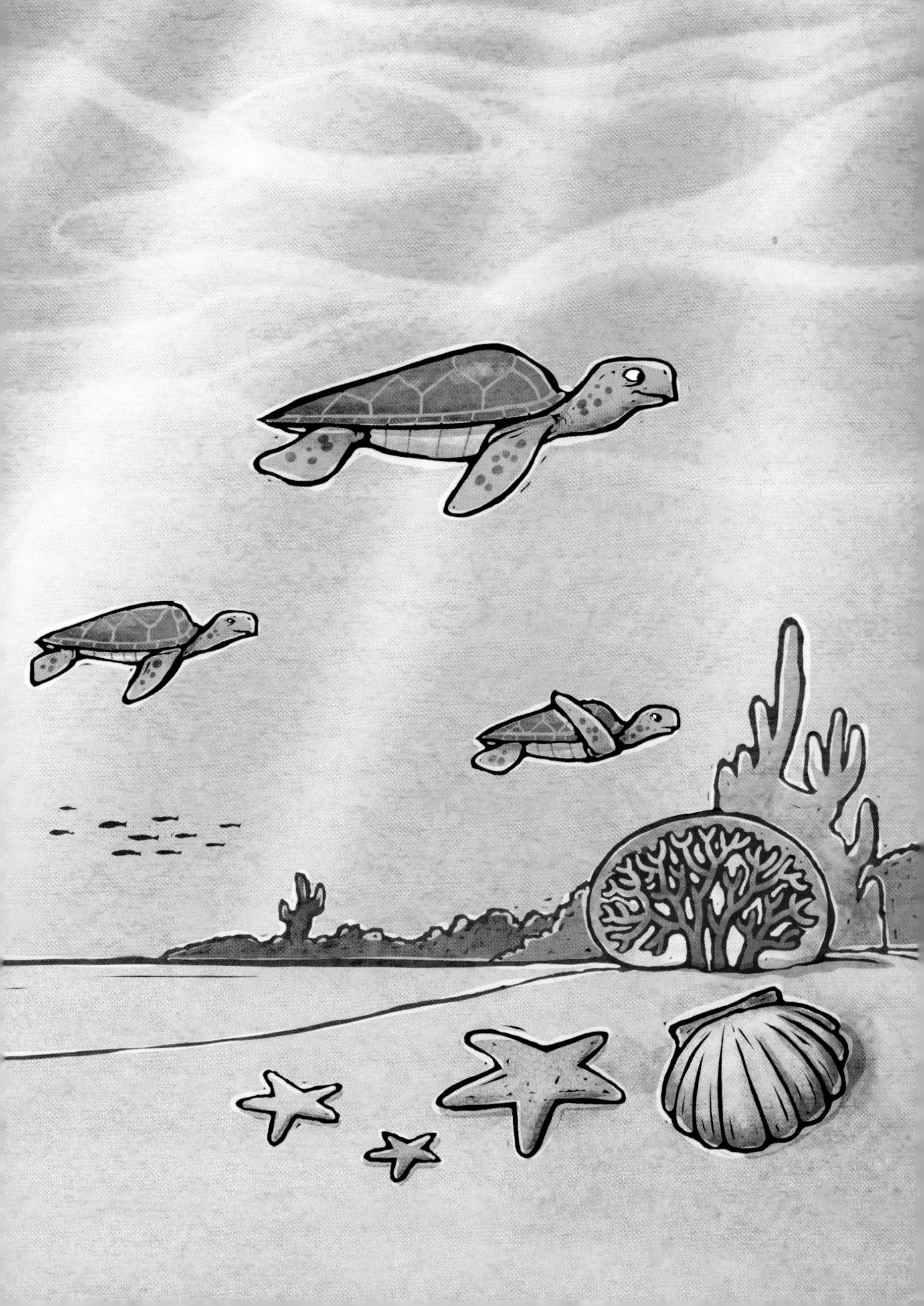

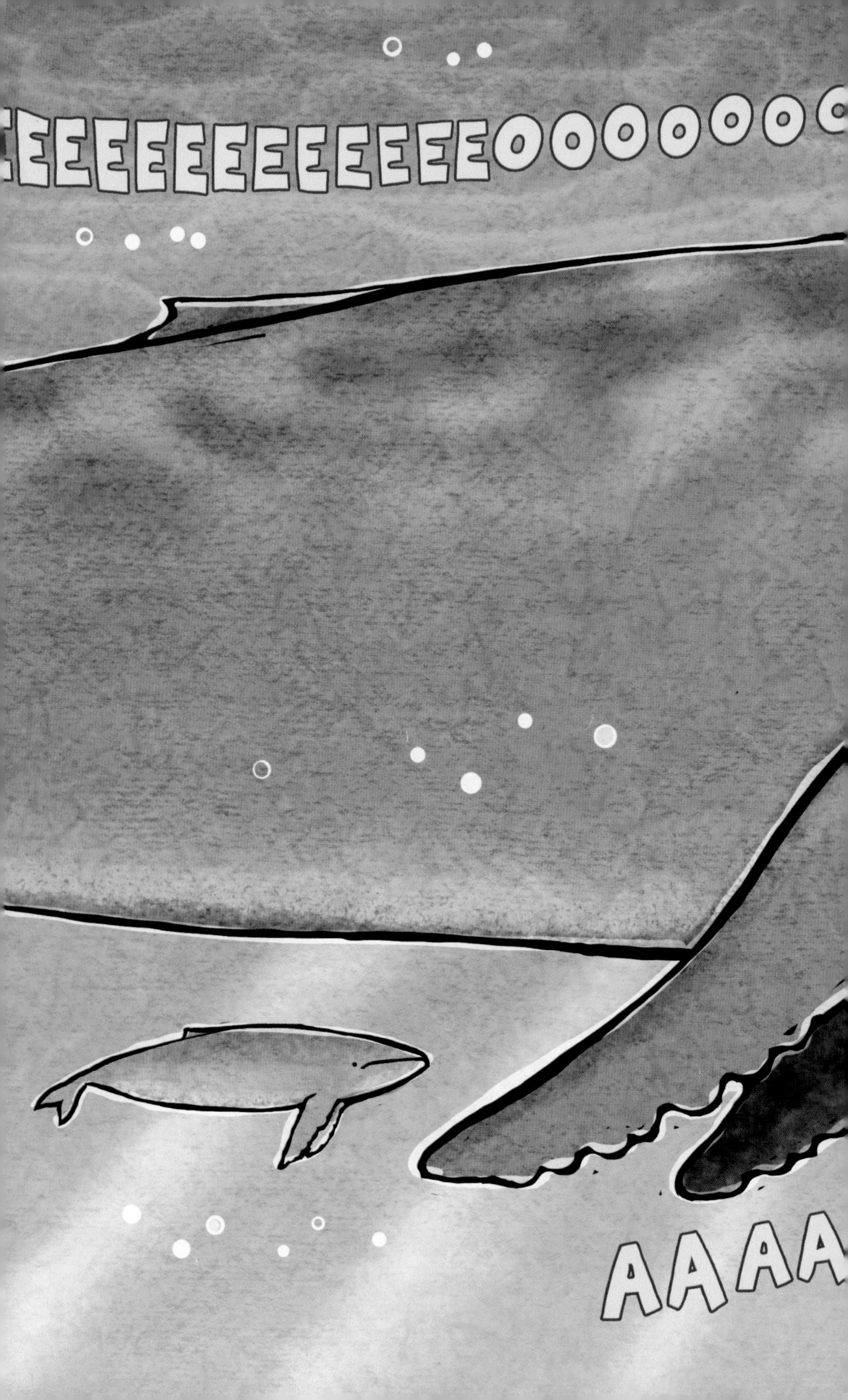
EEEEEEEEEEEEEOOOOOOO
AAAA

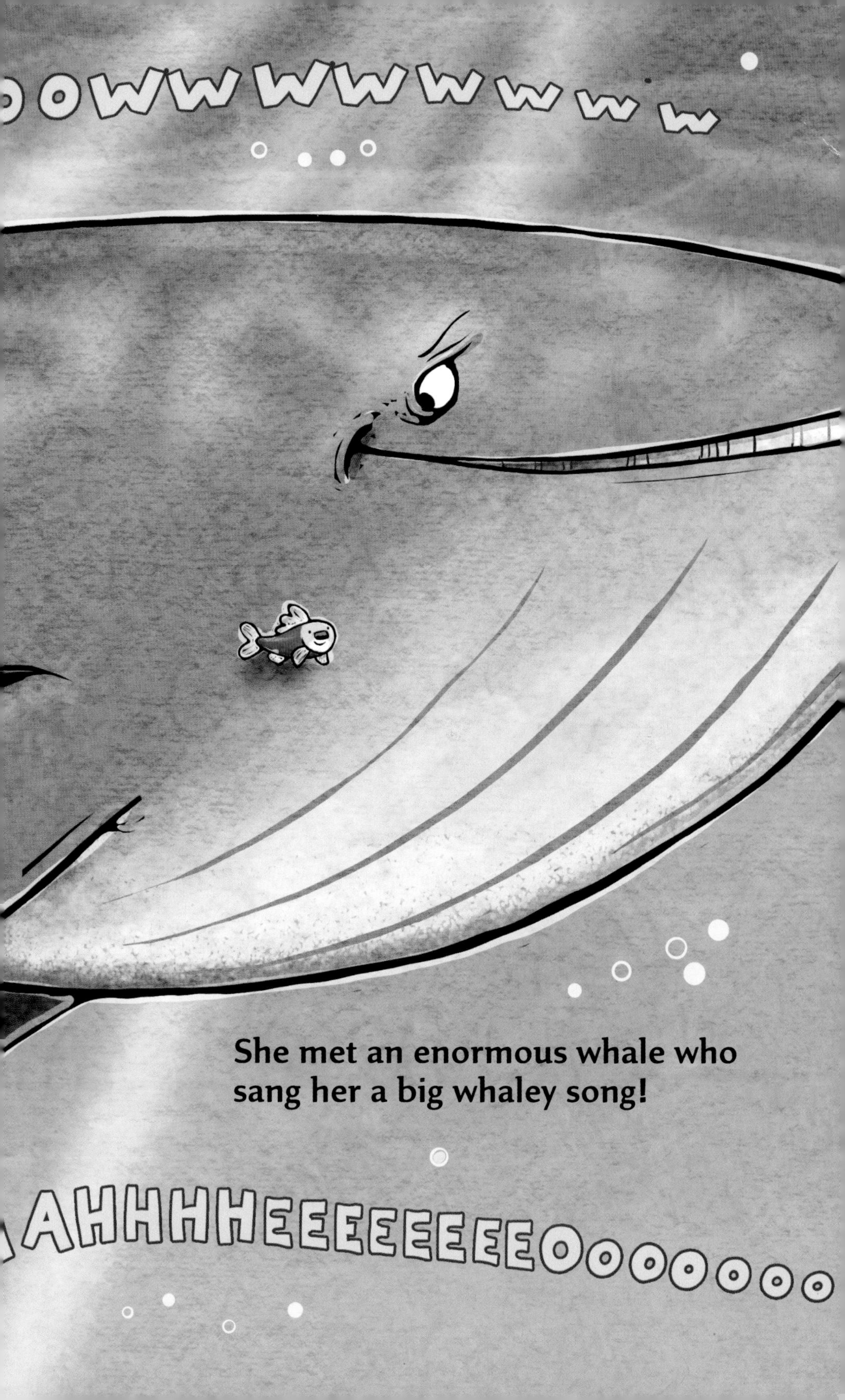
OOWWWWWWWW
AHHHHEEEEEEEEOOOOOOOO

She met an enormous whale who sang her a big whaley song!

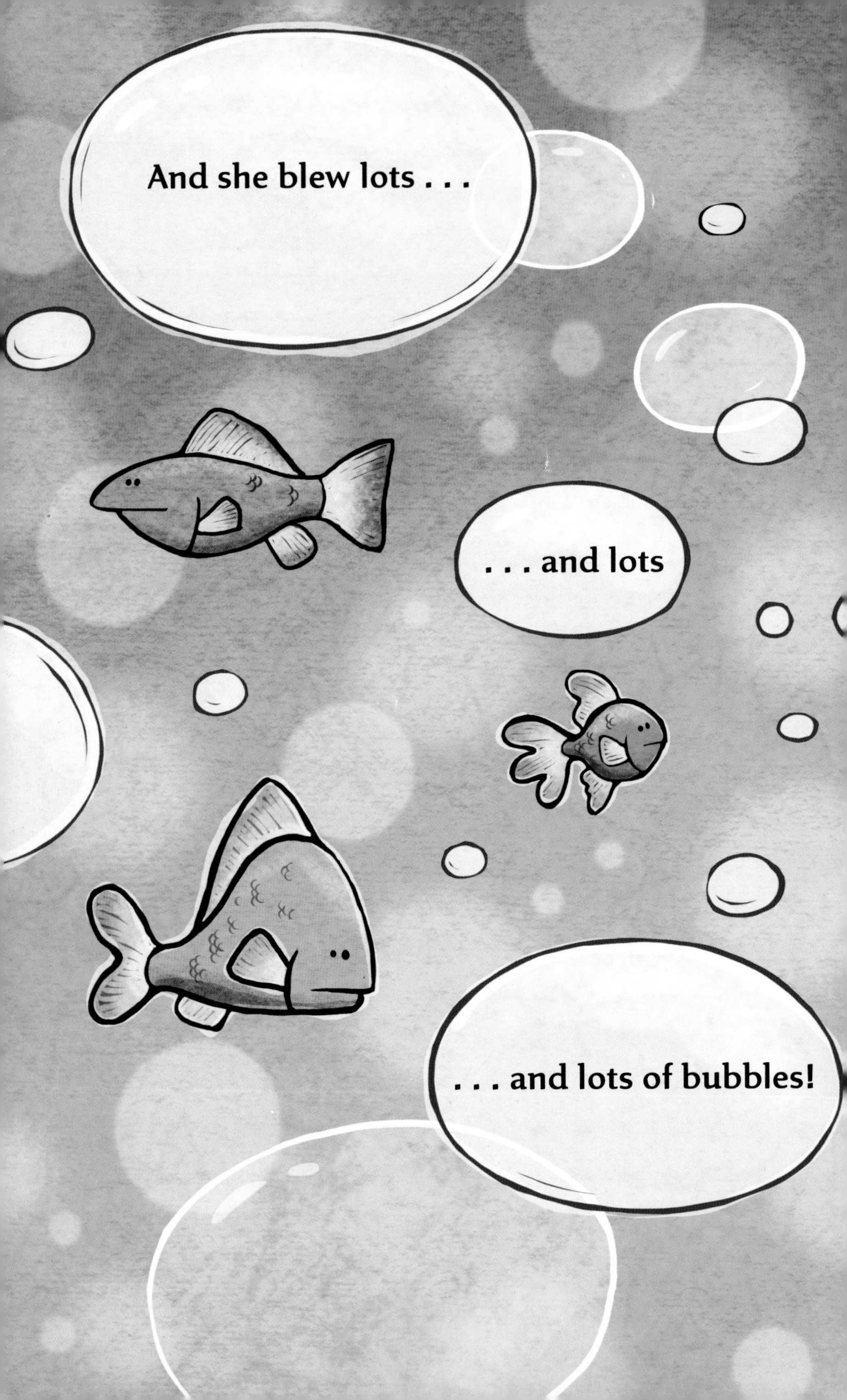
And she blew lots . . .
. . . and lots
. . . and lots of bubbles!

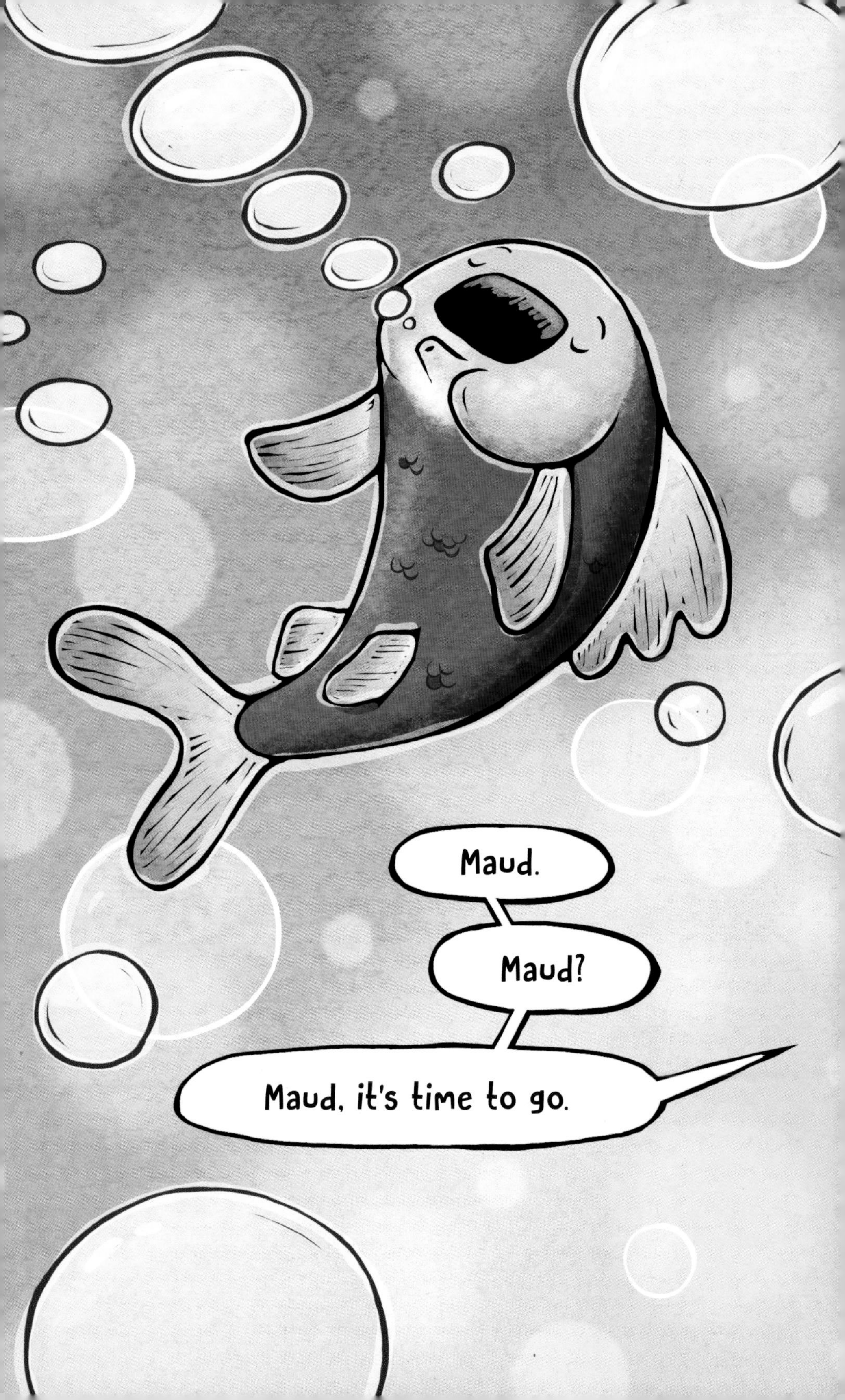
Maud.
Maud?
Maud, it's time to go.

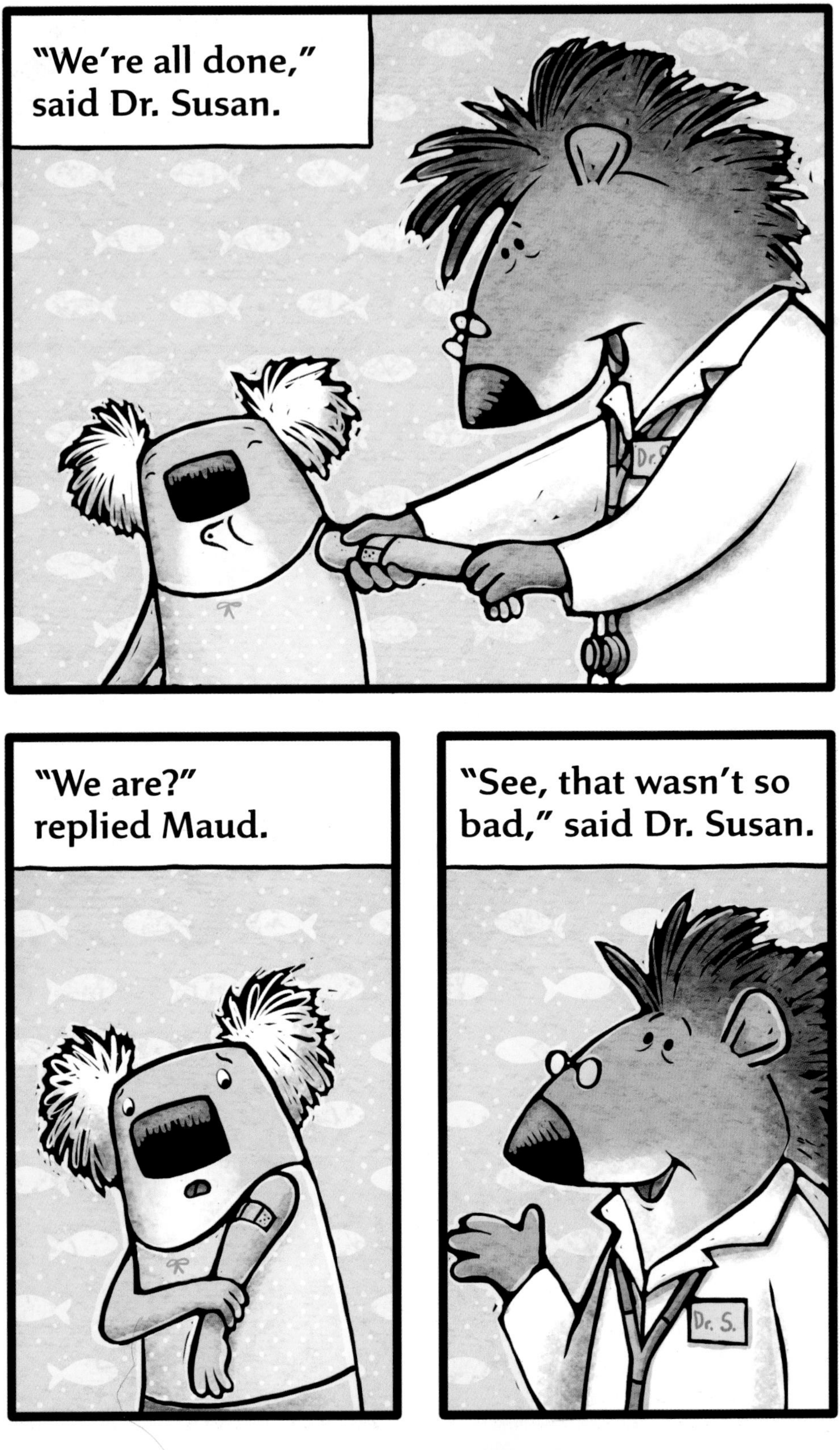
"We're all done," said Dr. Susan.
"We are?" replied Maud.
"See, that wasn't so bad," said Dr. Susan.
Dr. S.

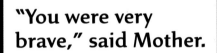
"Have a sticker."

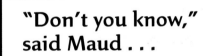
"You were very brave," said Mother.

"Don't you know," said Maud . . .

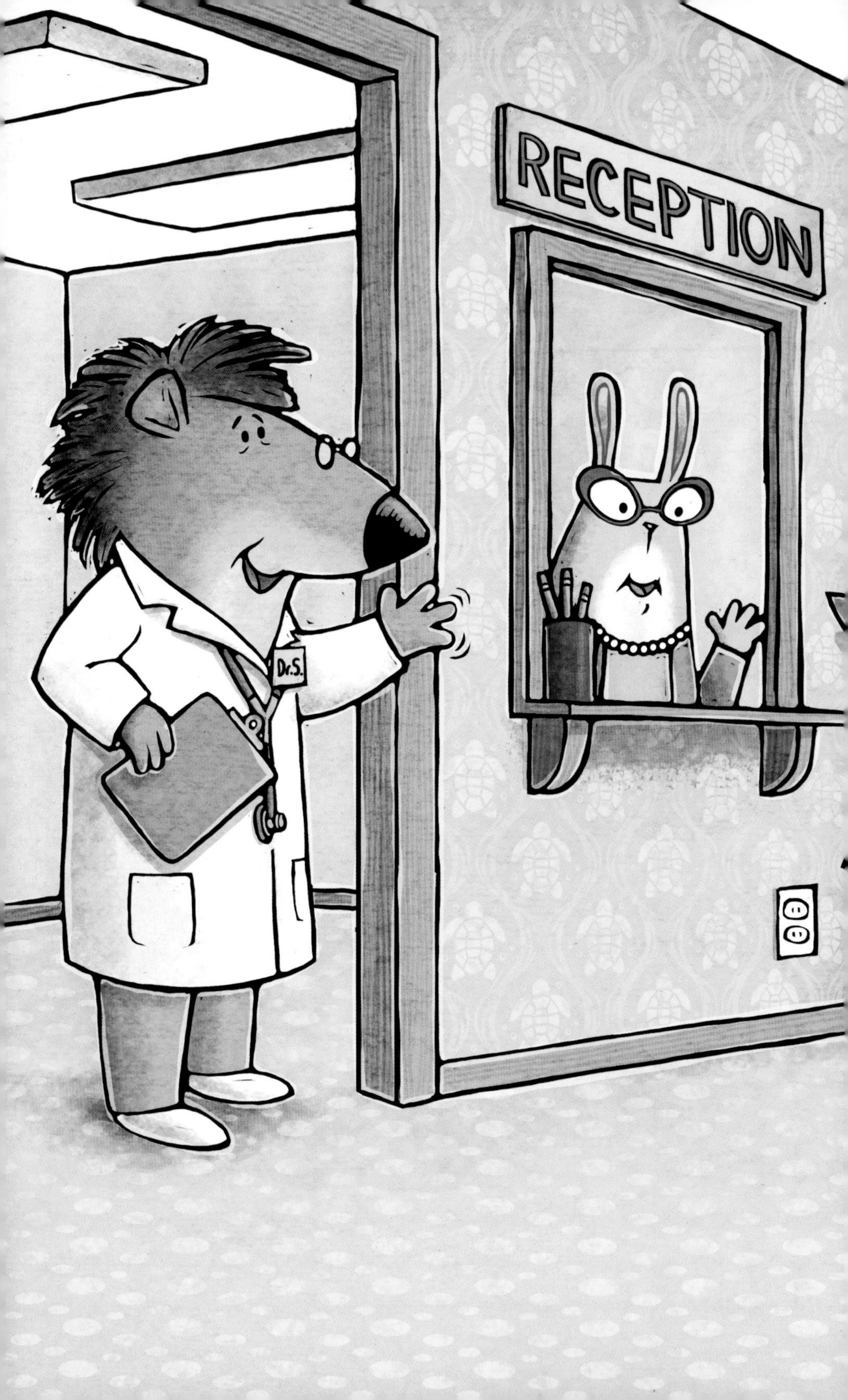
RECEPTION
Dr.S.

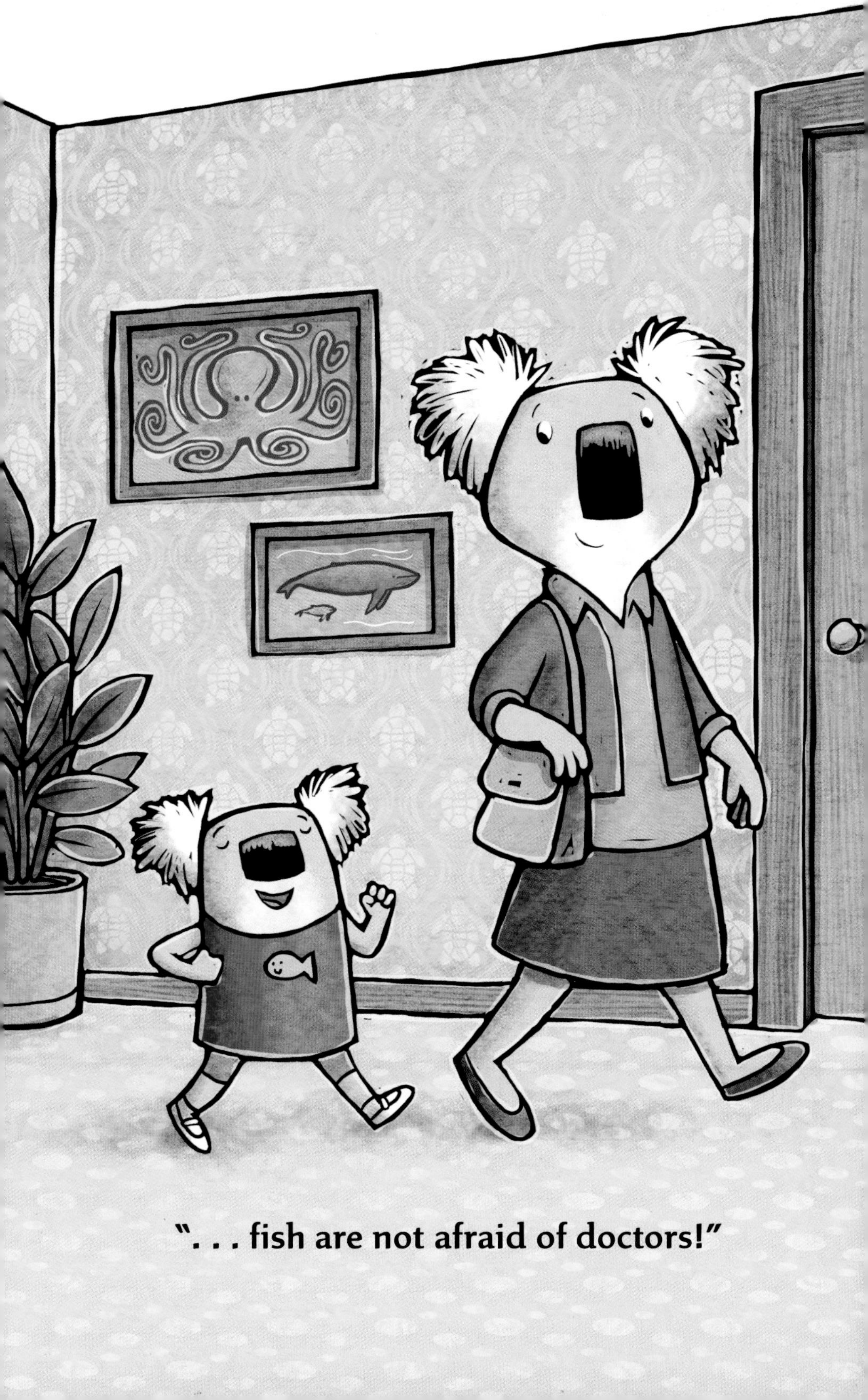

". . . fish are not afraid of doctors!"

Note to Caregivers

No one likes getting shots, but they are sometimes necessary to keep us healthy. Fear of needles is a common childhood anxiety. And as we adults know, the actual pain is usually not nearly as bad as the fear and apprehension leading up to it.

Visualization is an effective strategy for reducing the stress and anxiety. Pretending to be in a soothing place, like swimming through a colorful coral reef, can help relieve tension and calm a child's mind. Encourage children to use all of their senses to help them visualize their happy place. What would they see, hear, smell, and feel if they were really there?

Blowing bubbles is another strategy for dealing with anxiety. Studies have shown that children who have been distracted by blowing bubbles during injections have reported less pain. Blowing on a toy pinwheel, blowing soap bubbles, or just pretending to blow bubbles are all useful distractions.

Your child will most likely never look forward to getting a shot. But by using relaxation and distraction techniques, the process can be made less painful and traumatic for everyone involved.

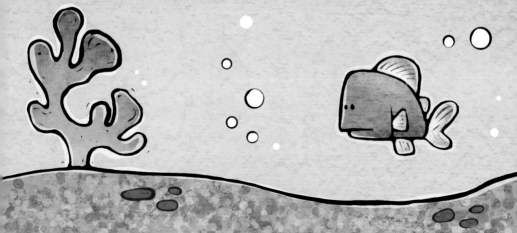

Much Too Much Birthday

by J. E. Morris

For you,
on your special day.
Happy birthday!

–JEM

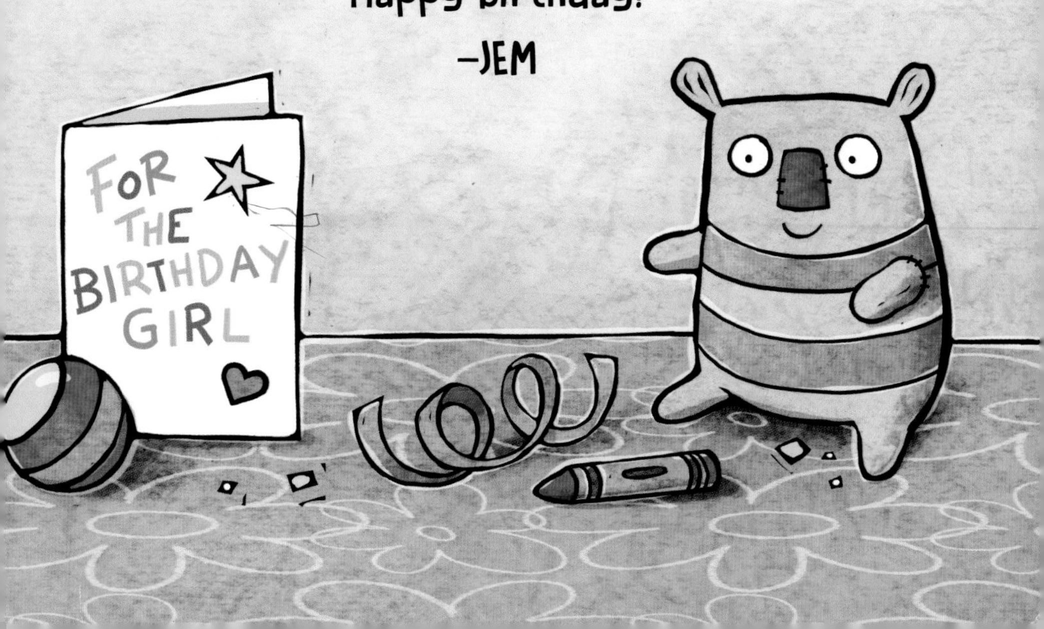
FOR THE BIRTHDAY GIRL

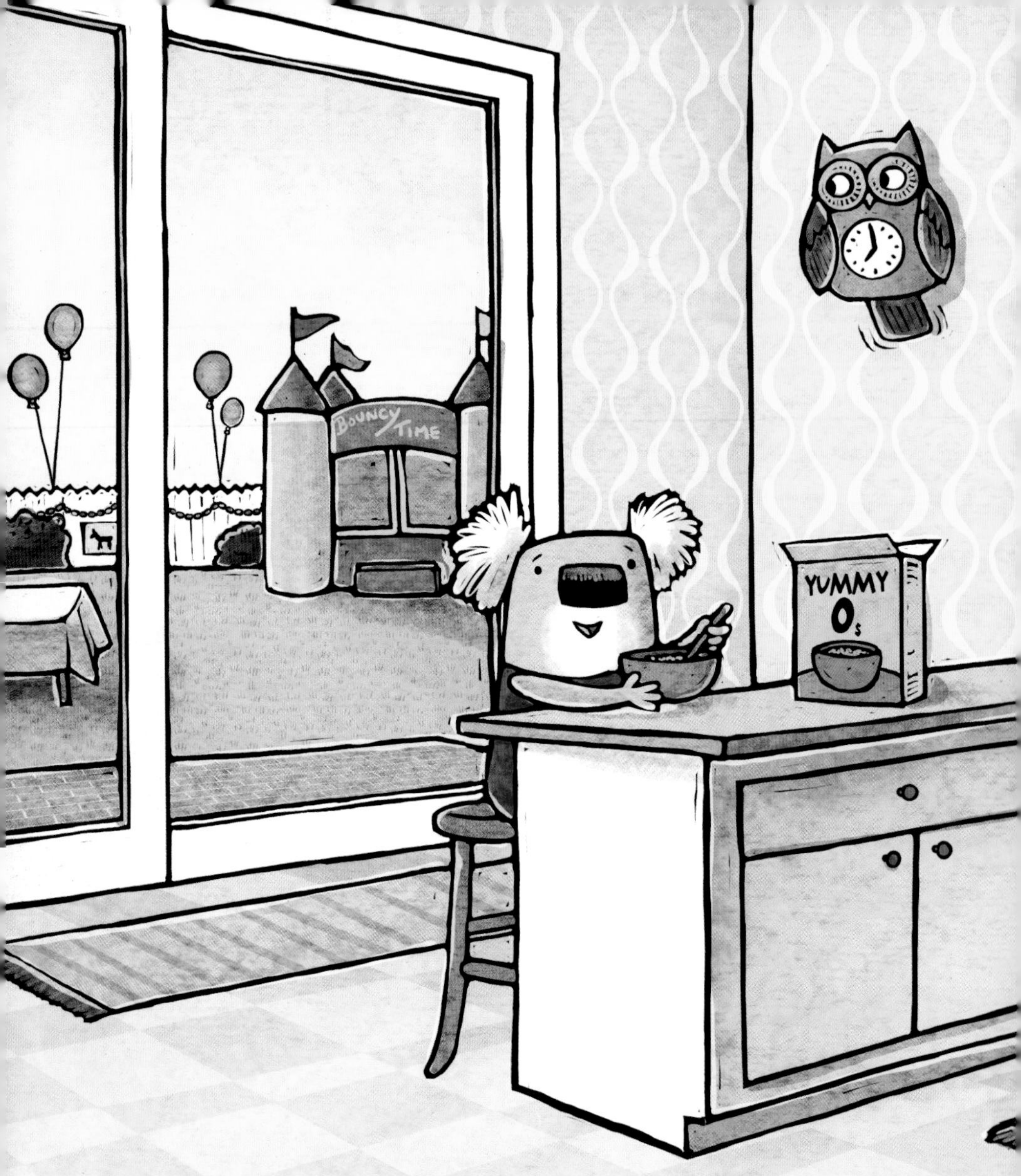
BOUNCY TIME
YUMMY
Os

Maud was very excited. Today was her birthday, and she had invited all her friends to help her celebrate.

"The guests will be here soon," said Mother. "Come help me decorate the cupcakes."

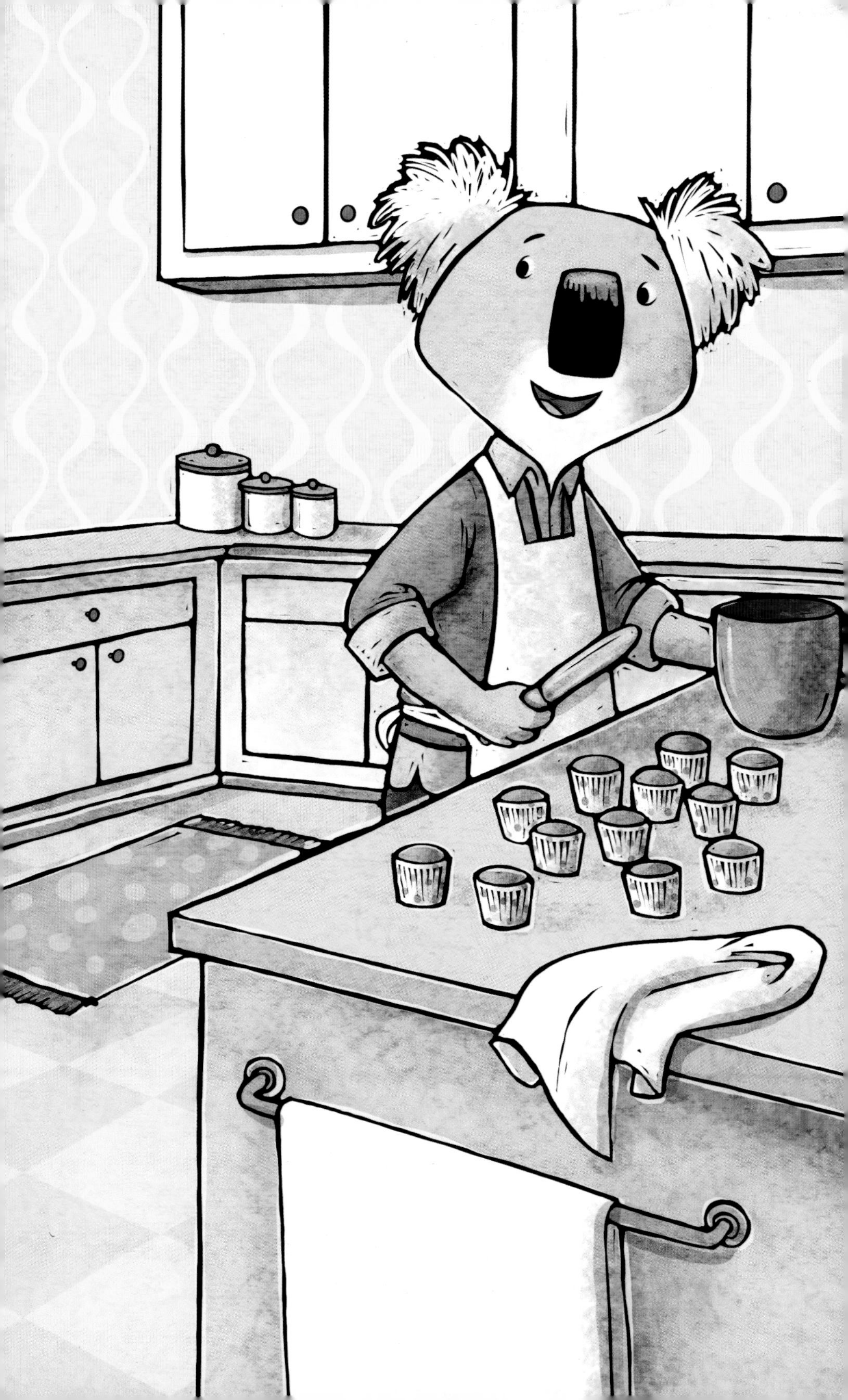

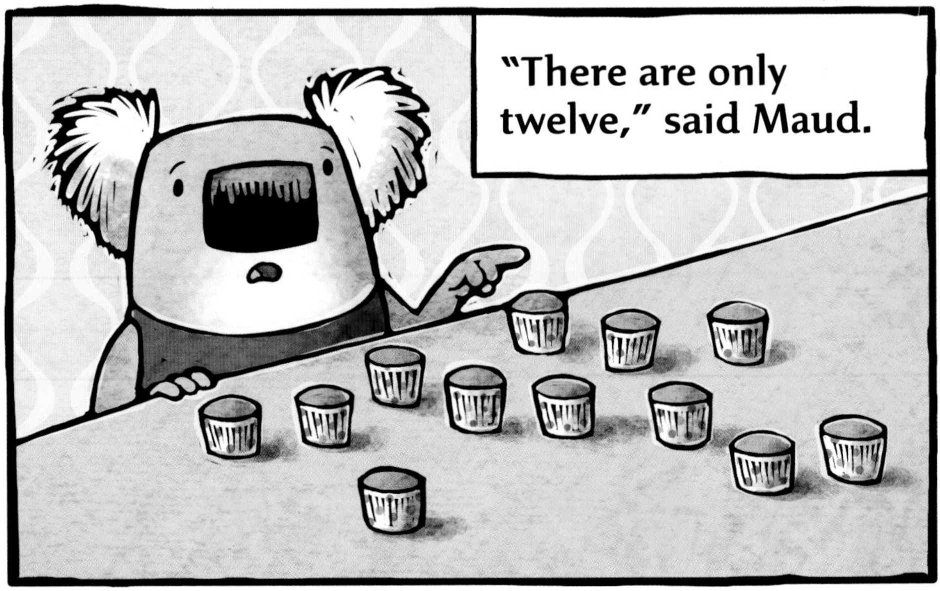
"There are only twelve," said Maud.

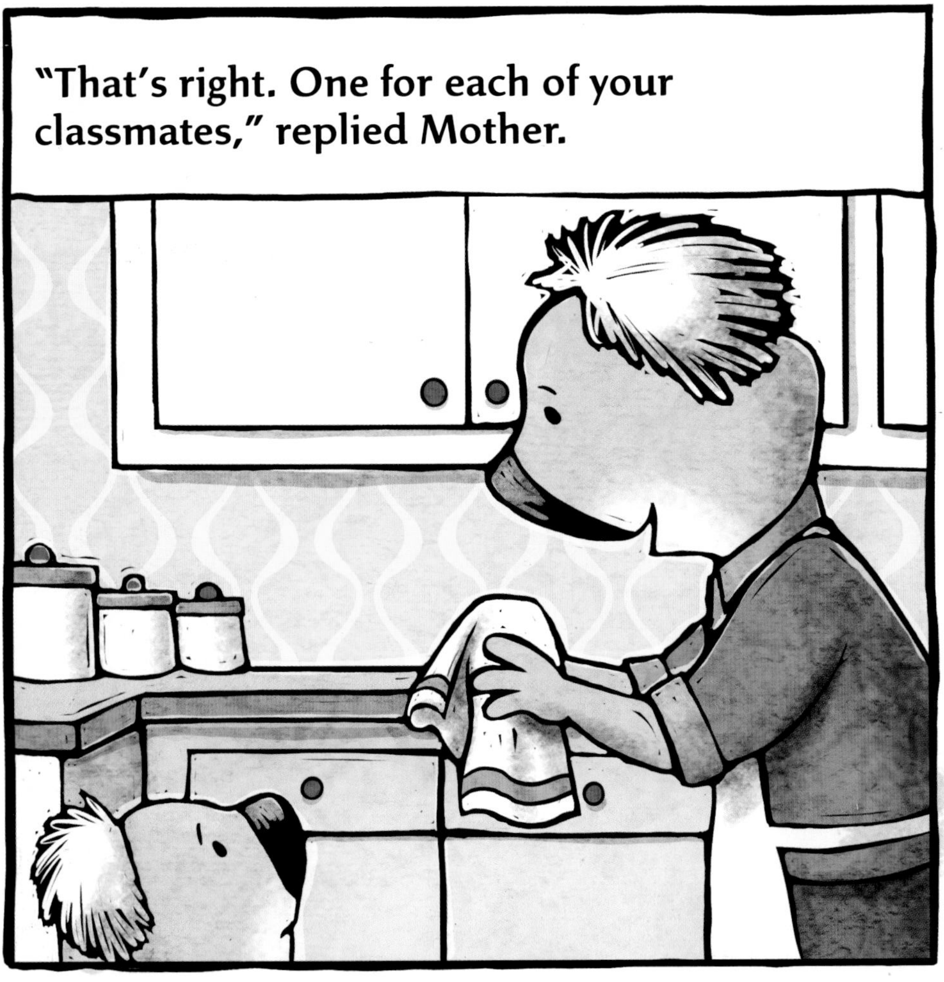
"That's right. One for each of your classmates," replied Mother.

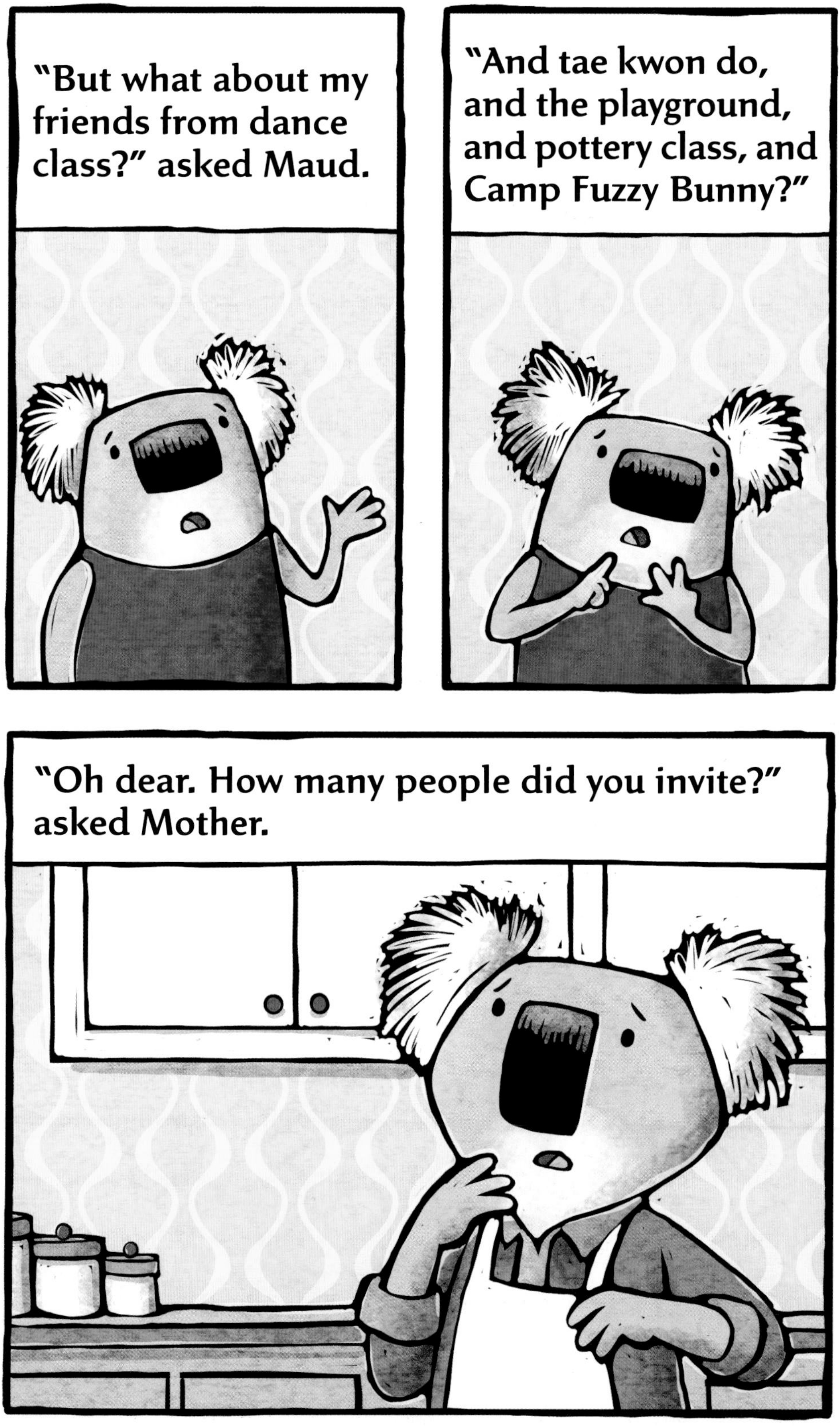
"But what about my friends from dance class?" asked Maud.
"And tae kwon do, and the playground, and pottery class, and Camp Fuzzy Bunny?"
"Oh dear. How many people did you invite?" asked Mother.

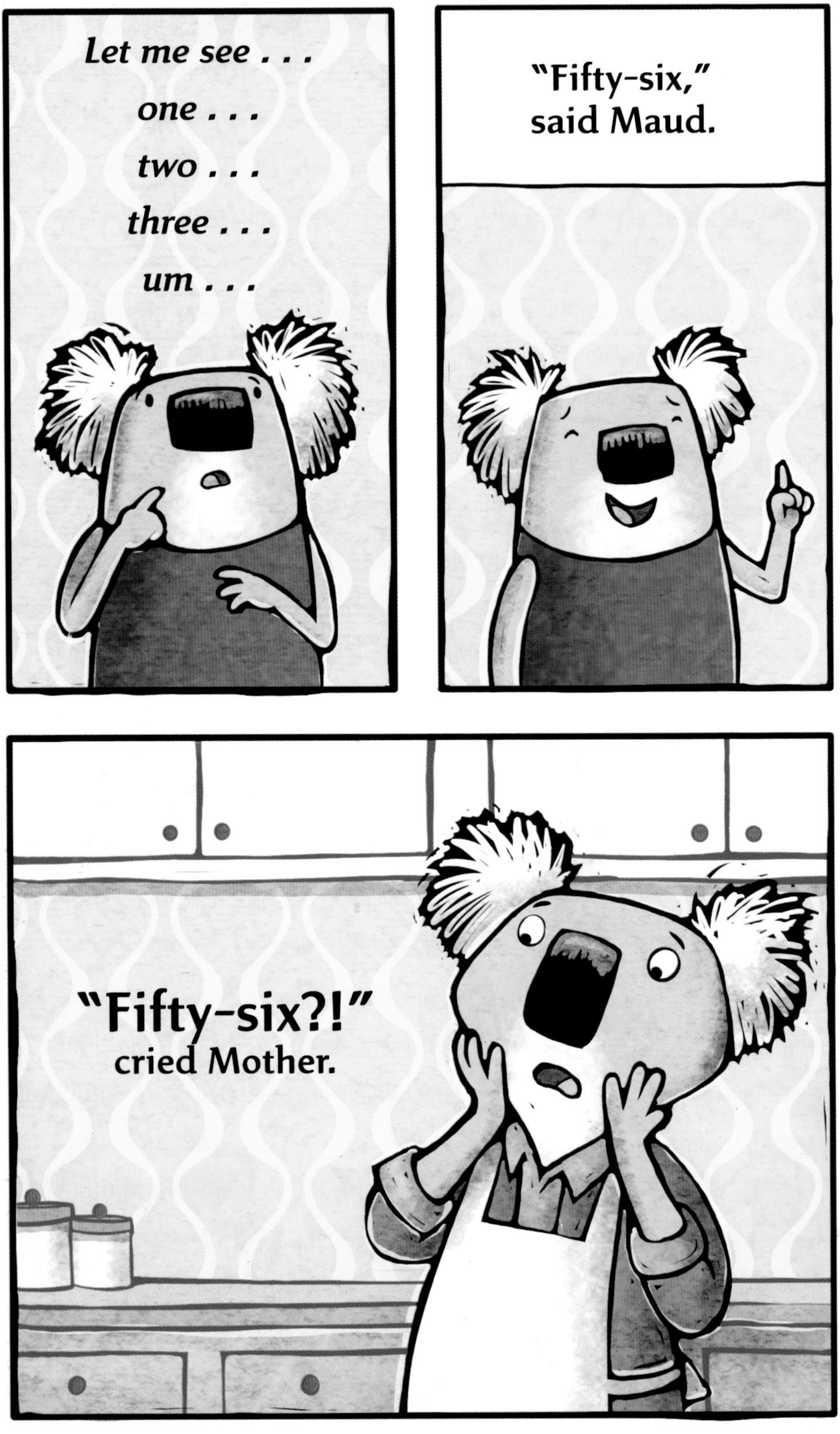
Let me see . . .
one . . .
two . . .
three . . .
um . . .
"Fifty-six,"
said Maud.
"Fifty-six?!"
cried Mother.

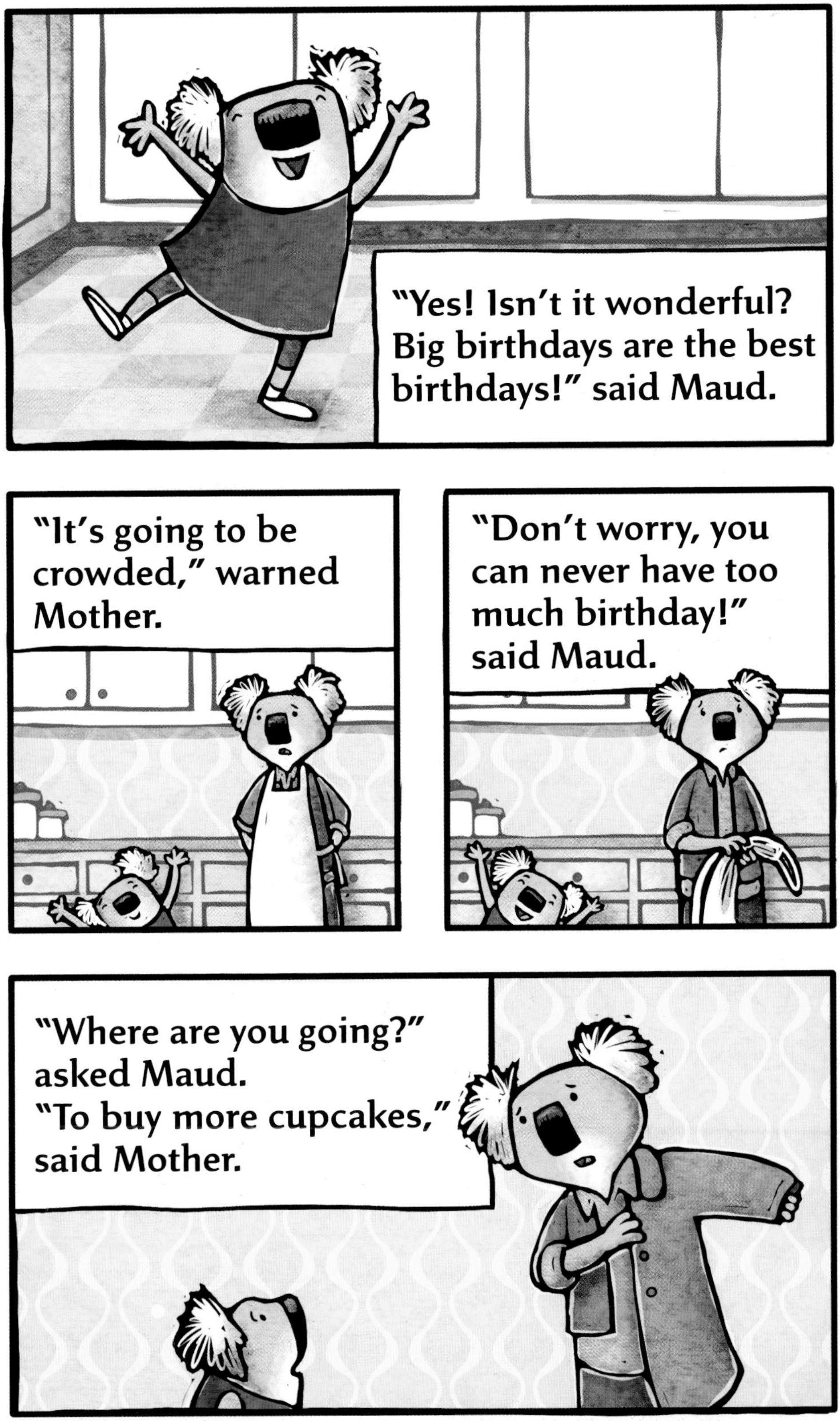
"Yes! Isn't it wonderful? Big birthdays are the best birthdays!" said Maud.
"It's going to be crowded," warned Mother.
"Don't worry, you can never have too much birthday!" said Maud.
"Where are you going?" asked Maud.
"To buy more cupcakes," said Mother.

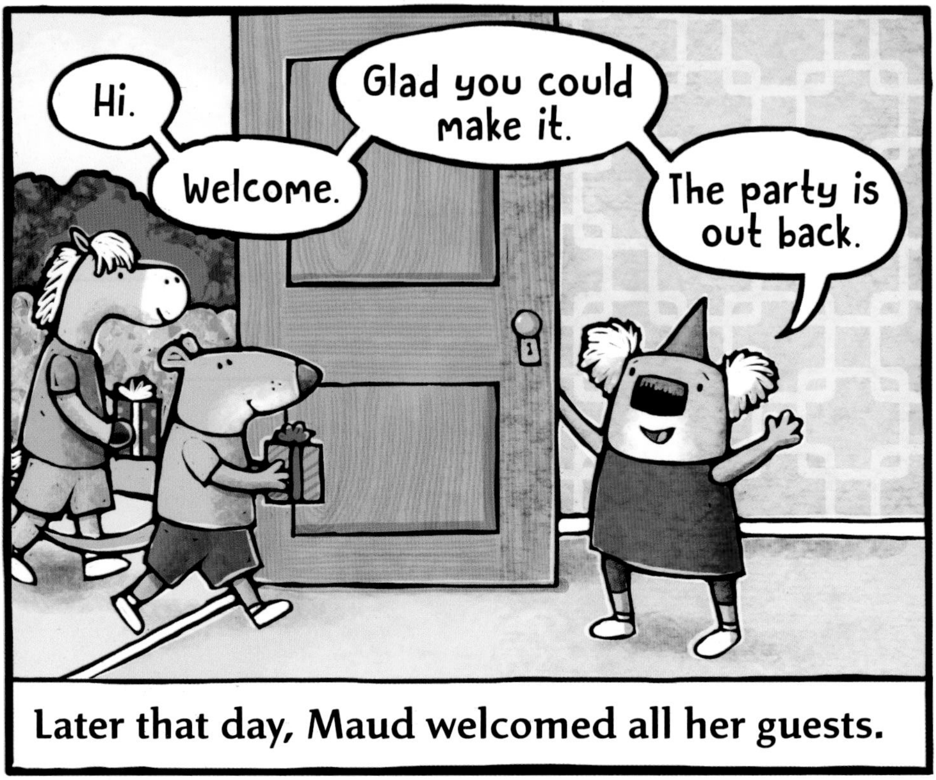
Hi.
Welcome.
Glad you could make it.
The party is out back.
Later that day, Maud welcomed all her guests.

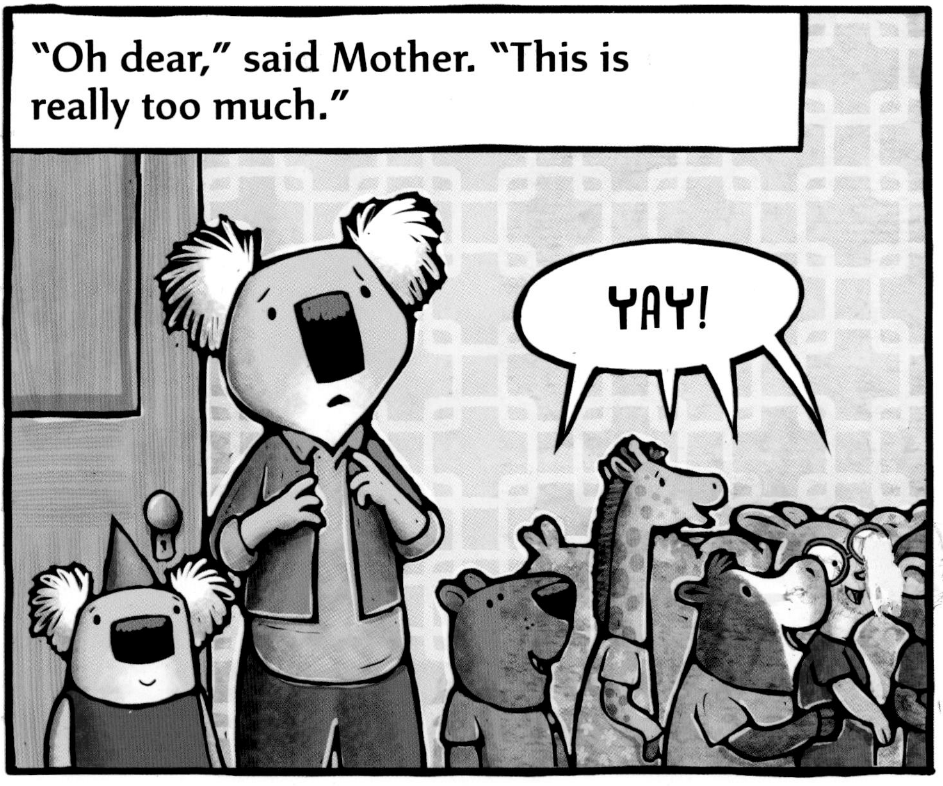
"Oh dear," said Mother. "This is really too much."
YAY!

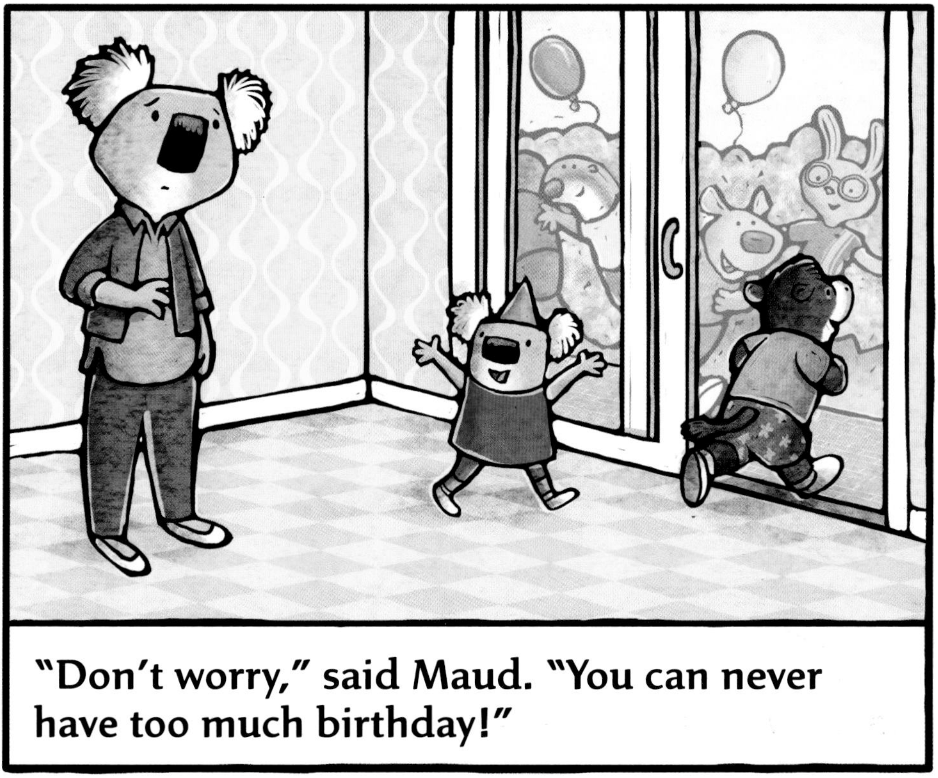
"Don't worry," said Maud. "You can never have too much birthday!"

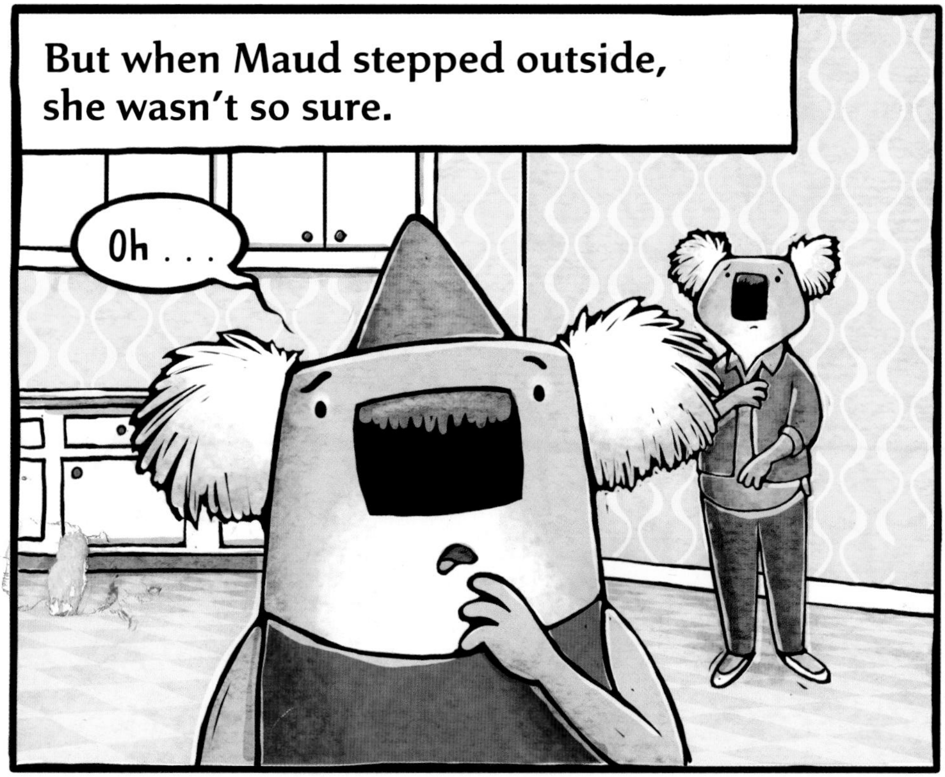
But when Maud stepped outside, she wasn't so sure.
Oh . . .

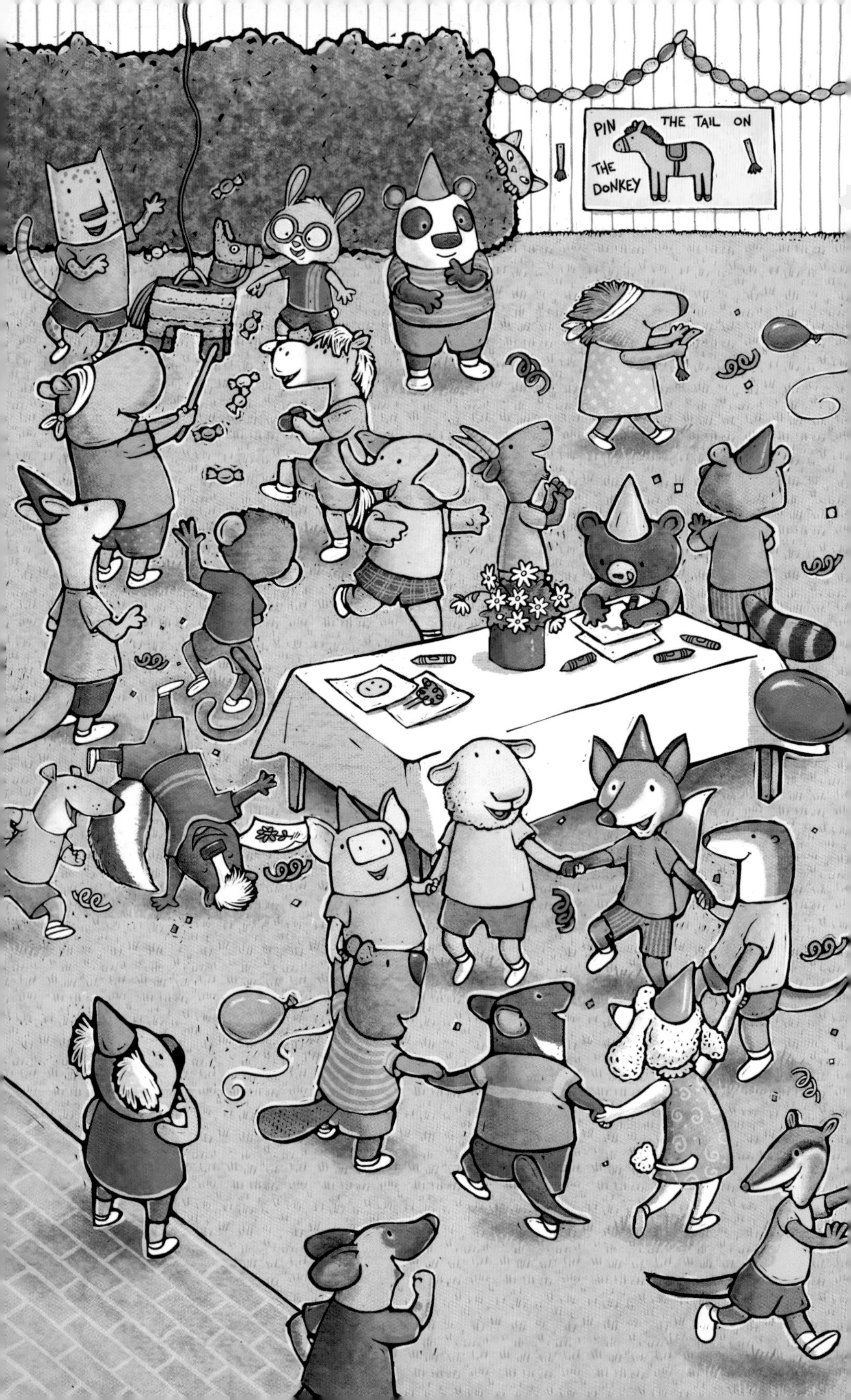
PIN THE TAIL ON THE DONKEY

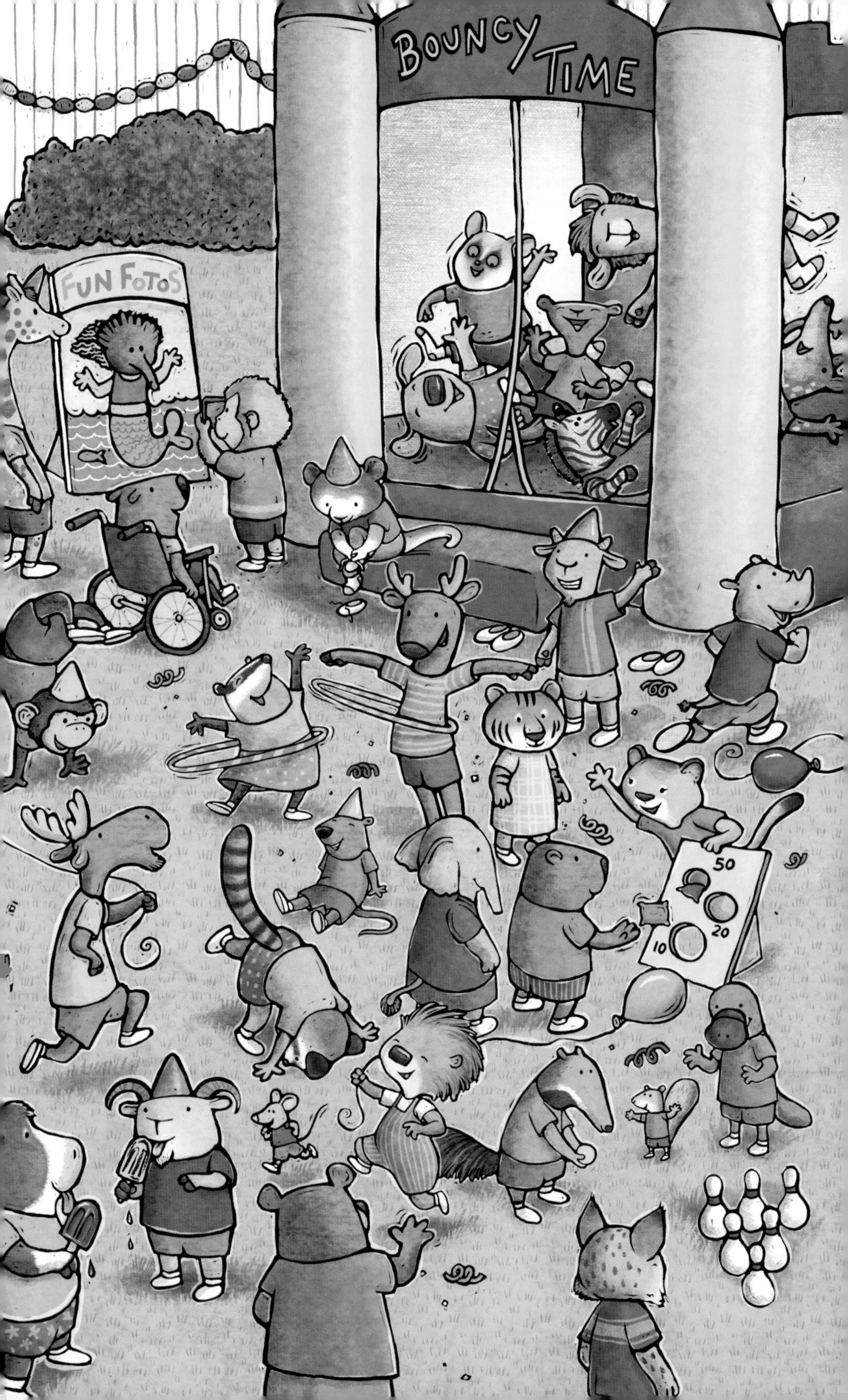
BOUNCY TIME
FUN FOTOS
50
20
10

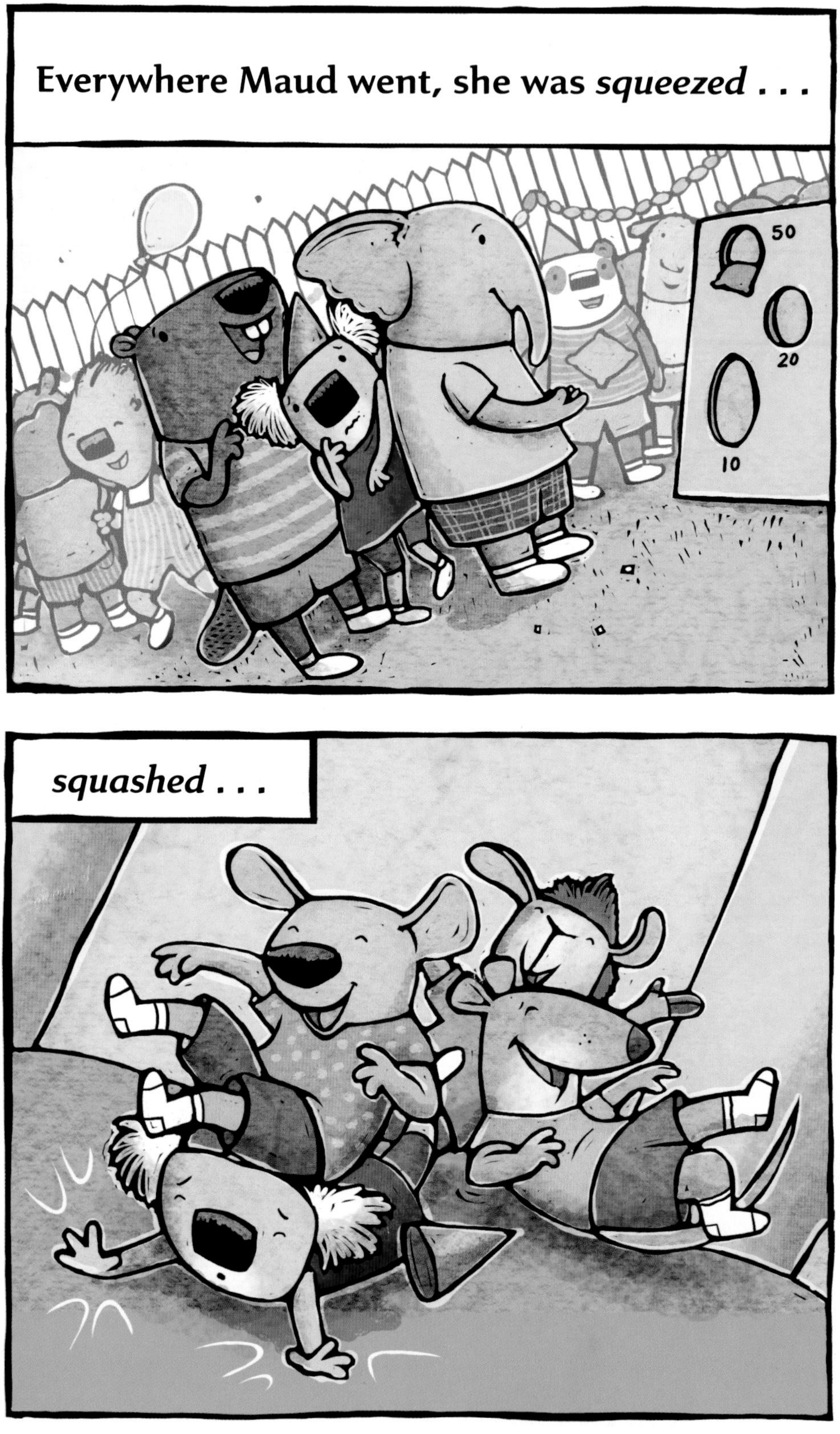
Everywhere Maud went, she was *squeezed* . . .
50
20
10
squashed . . .

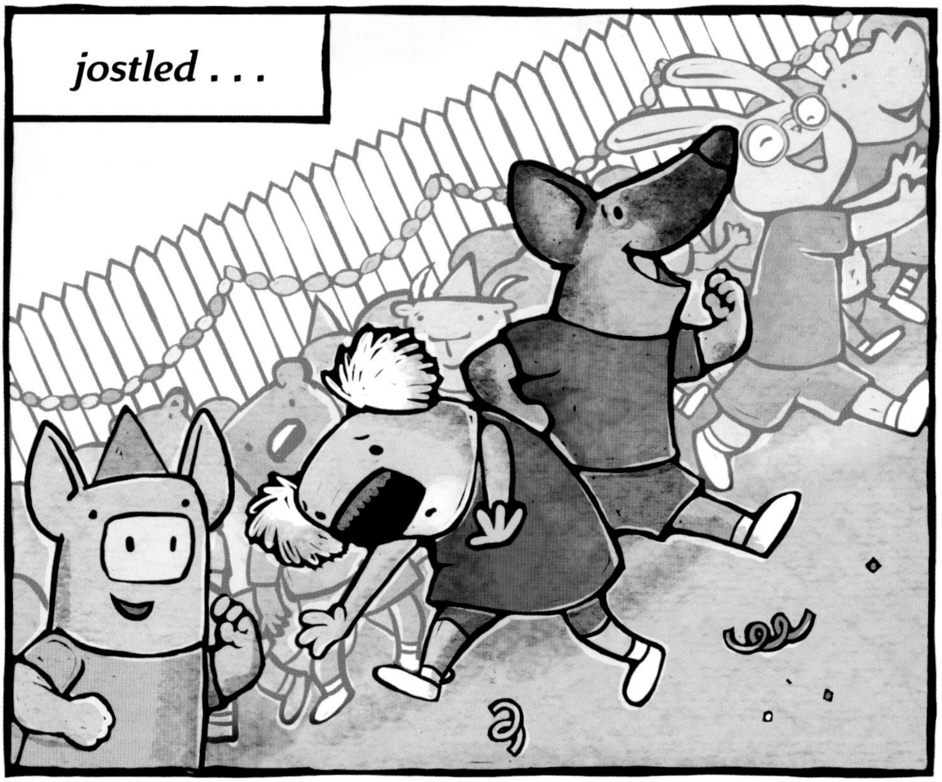
jostled . . .

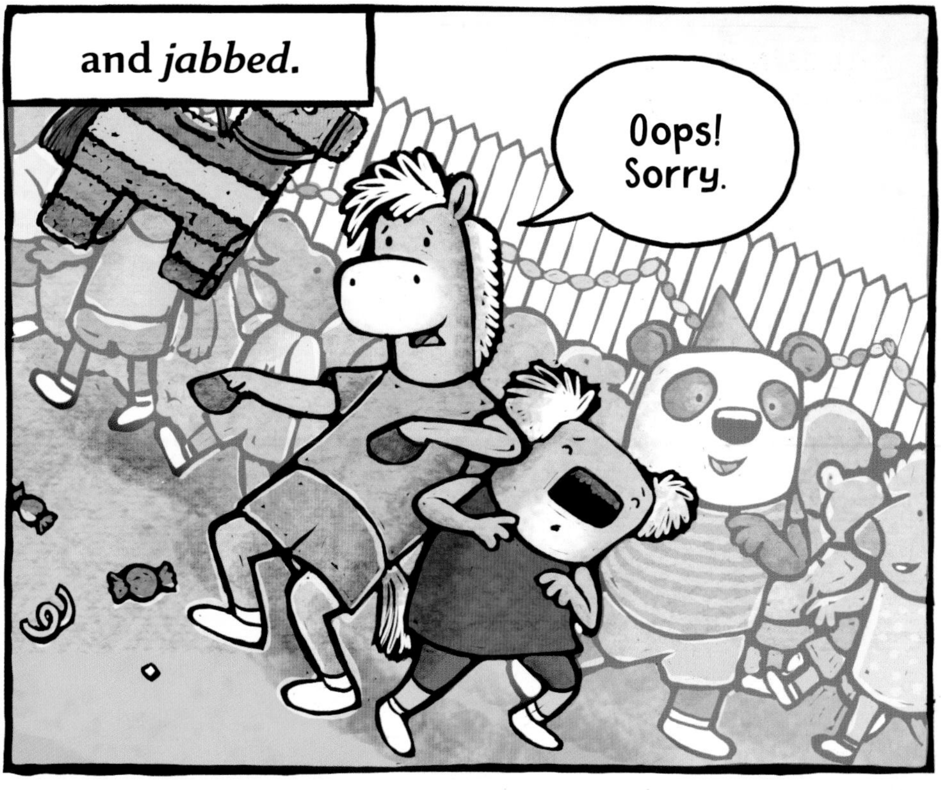
and jabbed.
Oops! Sorry.

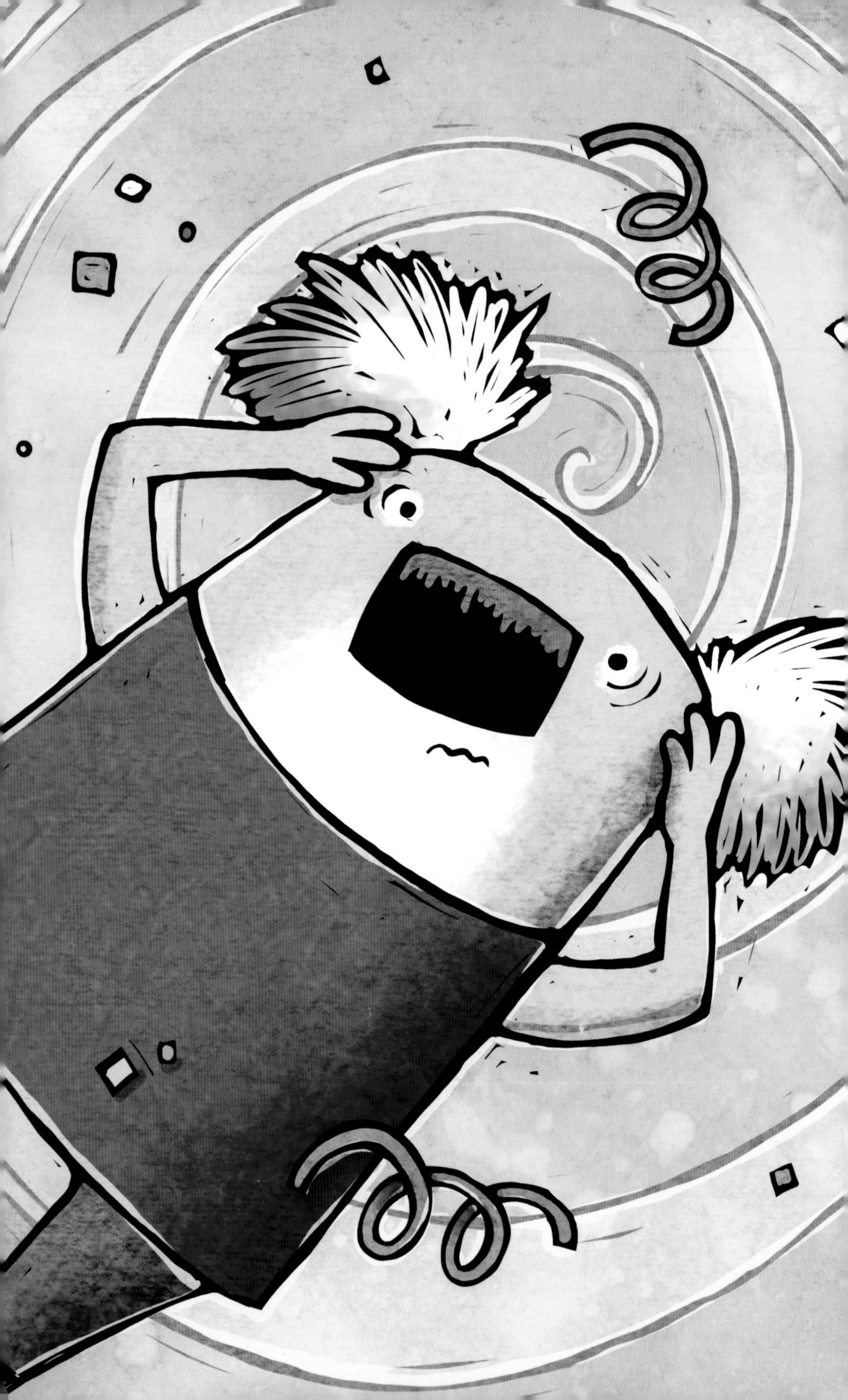

This wasn't at all what Maud had expected. Her tummy was queasy, and her head felt all floaty.

Quietly, Maud slipped behind the bushes.

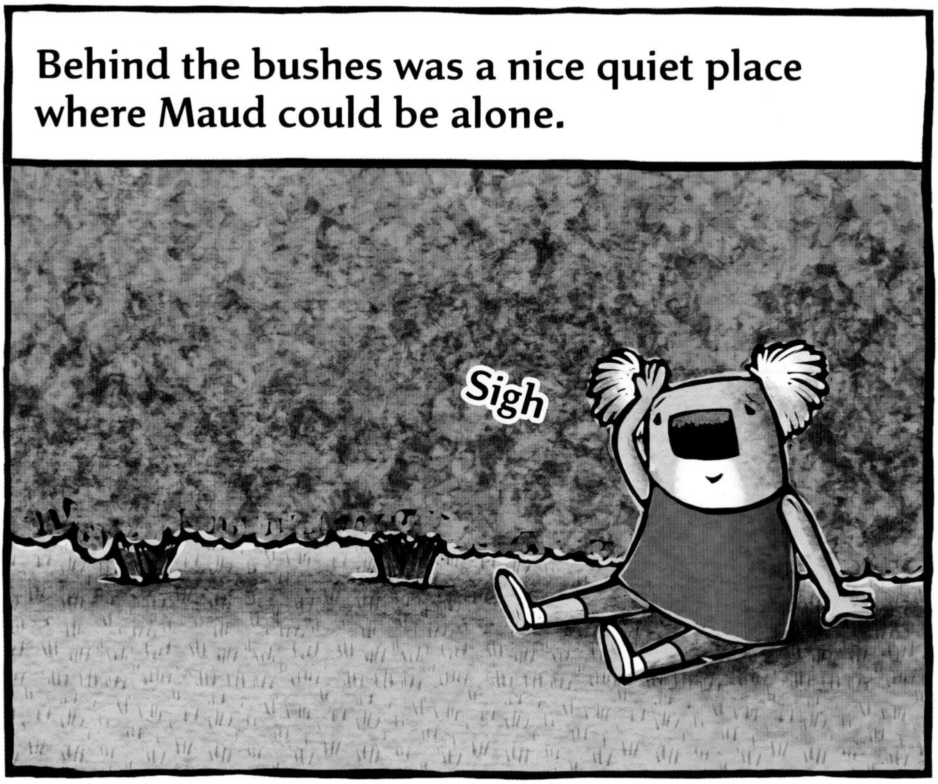
Behind the bushes was a nice quiet place where Maud could be alone.
Sigh

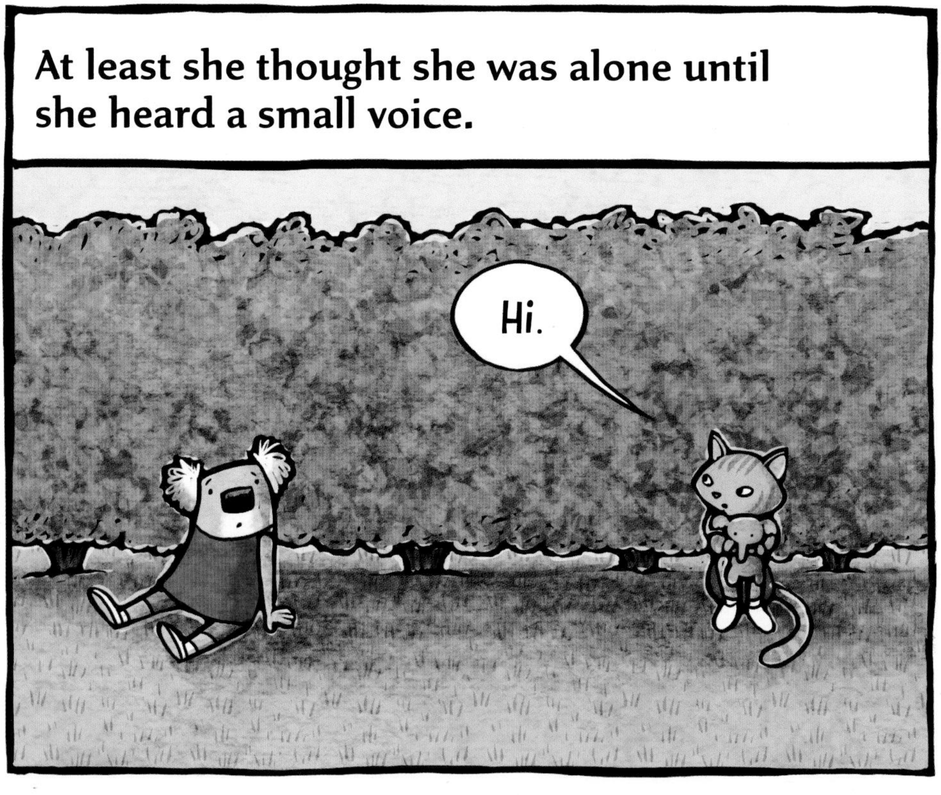
At least she thought she was alone until she heard a small voice.
Hi.

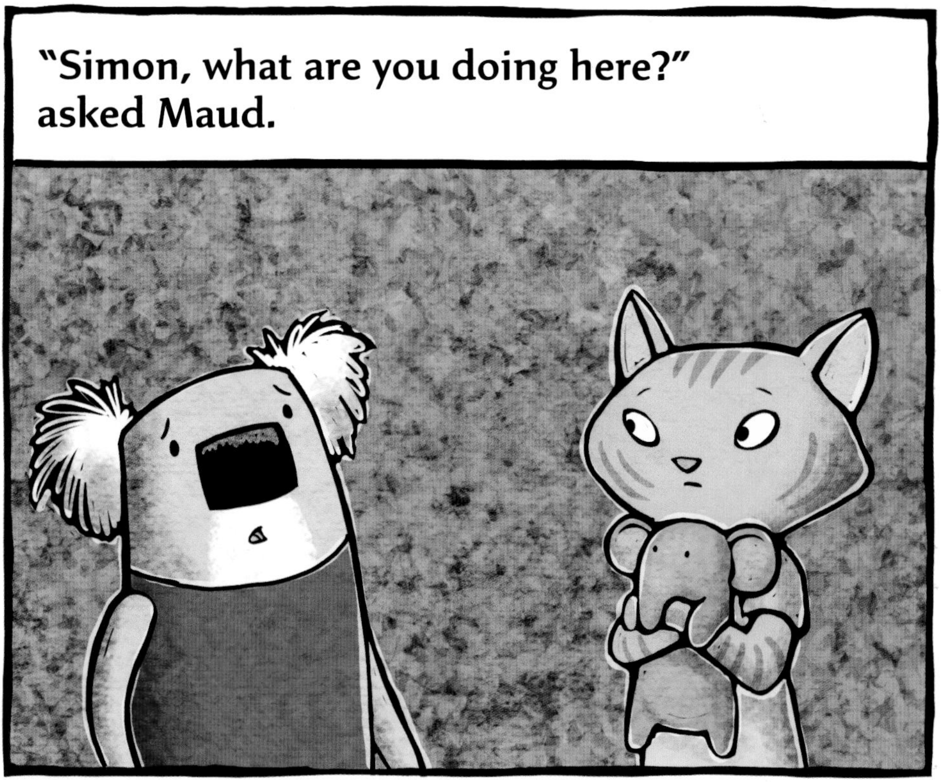
"Simon, what are you doing here?" asked Maud.

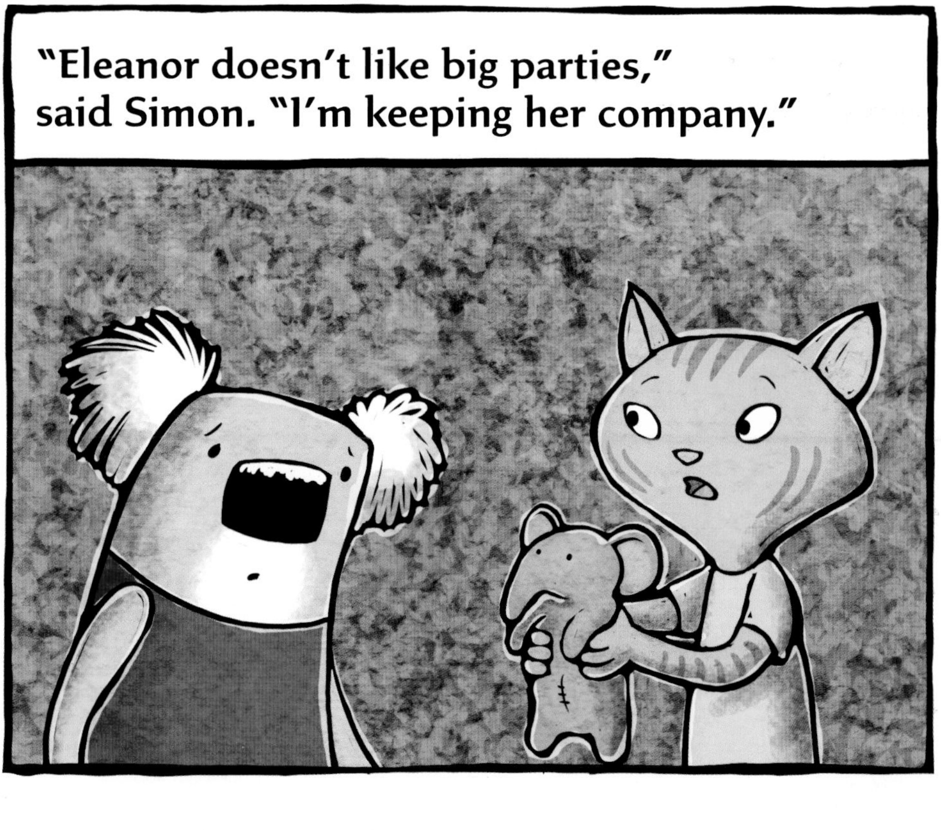
"Eleanor doesn't like big parties," said Simon. "I'm keeping her company."

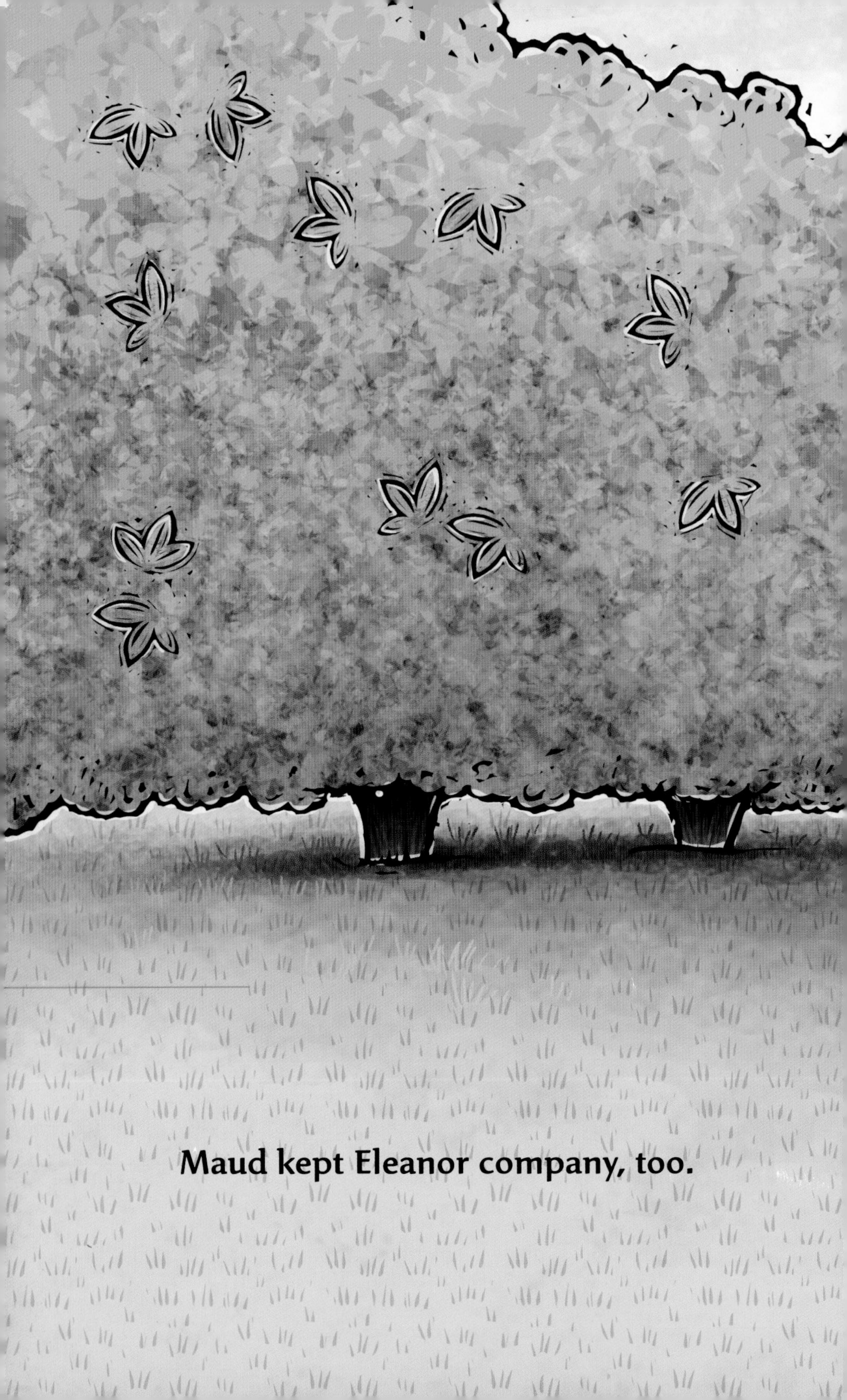

Maud kept Eleanor company, too.

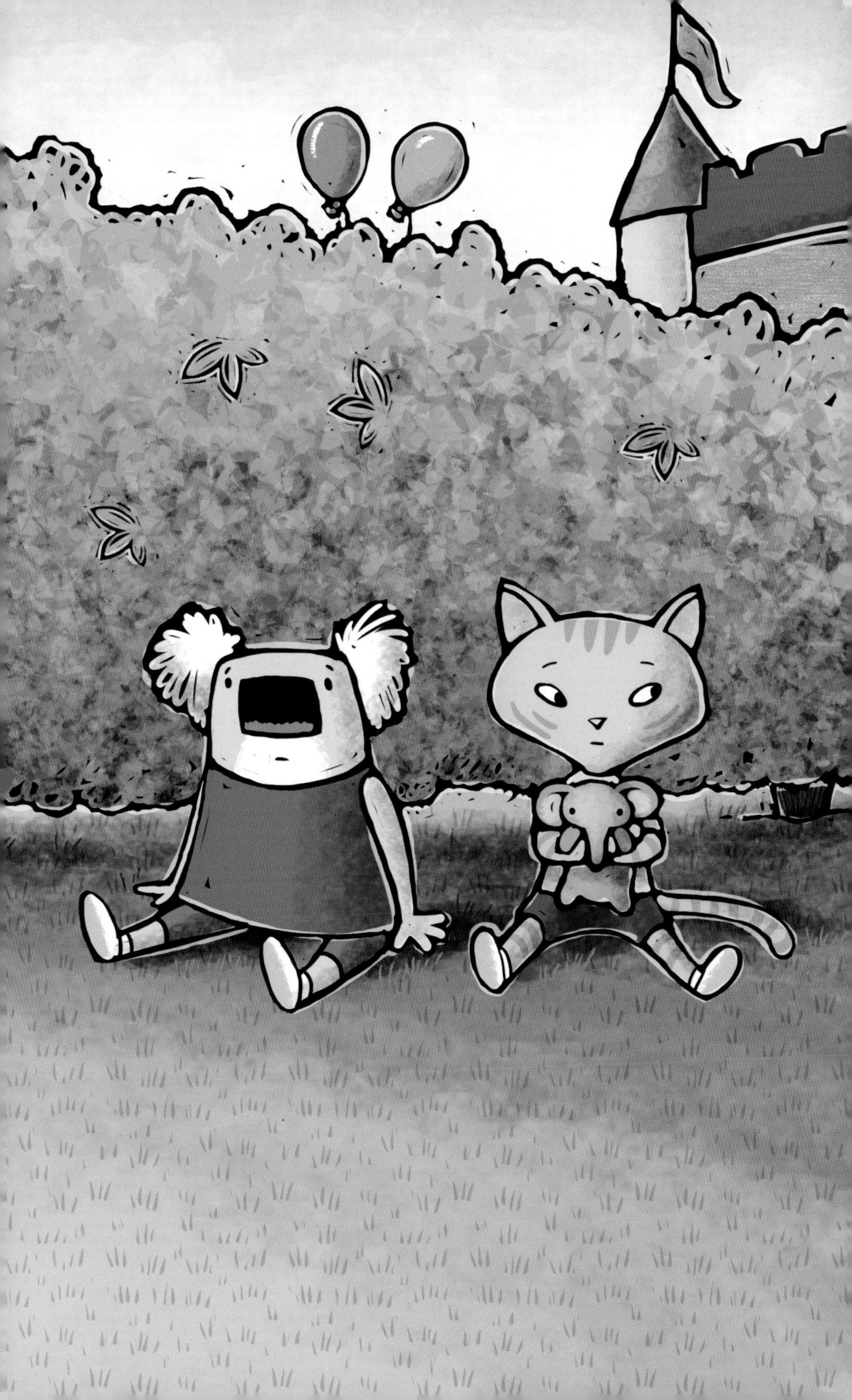

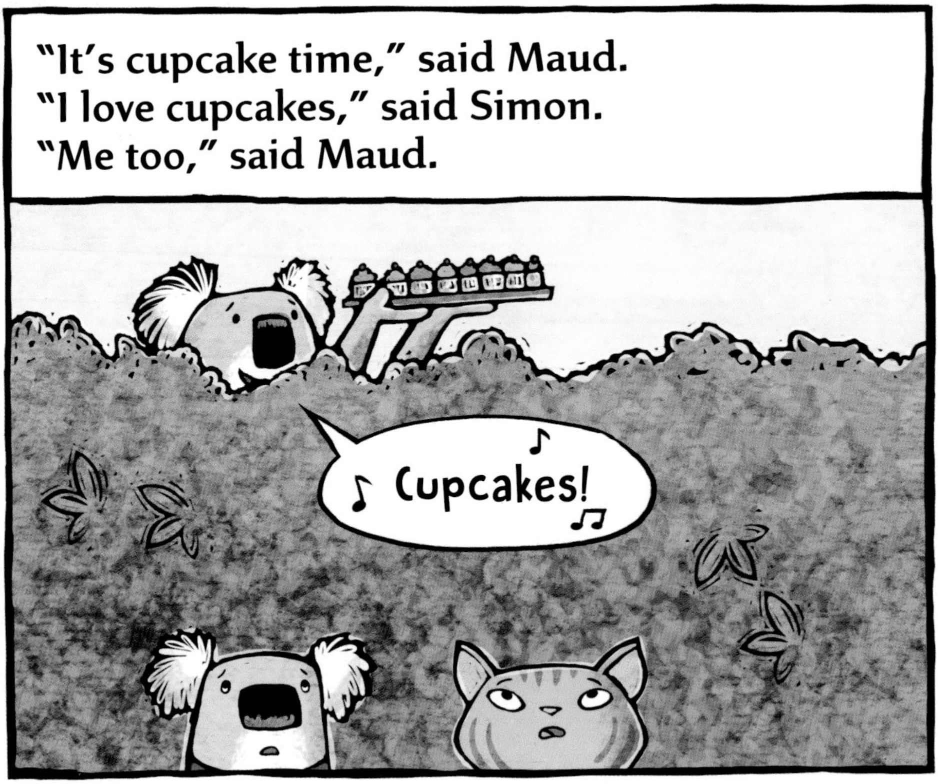
"It's cupcake time," said Maud.
"I love cupcakes," said Simon.
"Me too," said Maud.
Cupcakes!

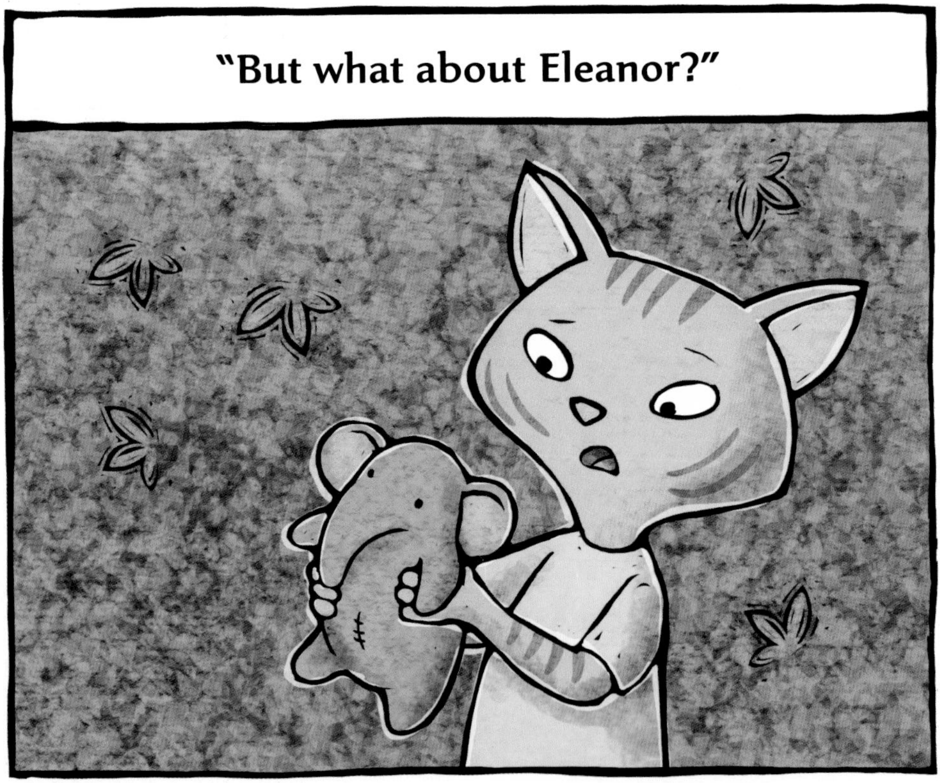
"But what about Eleanor?"

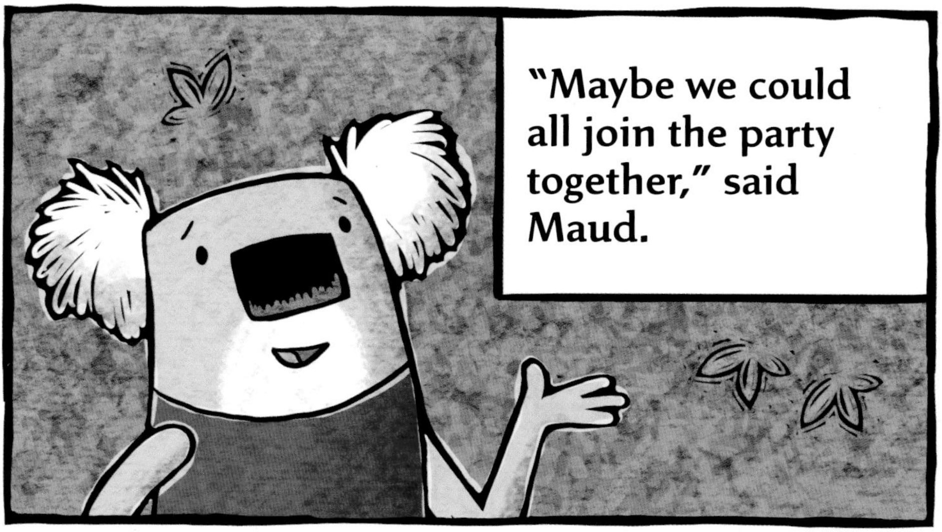
"Maybe we could all join the party together," said Maud.

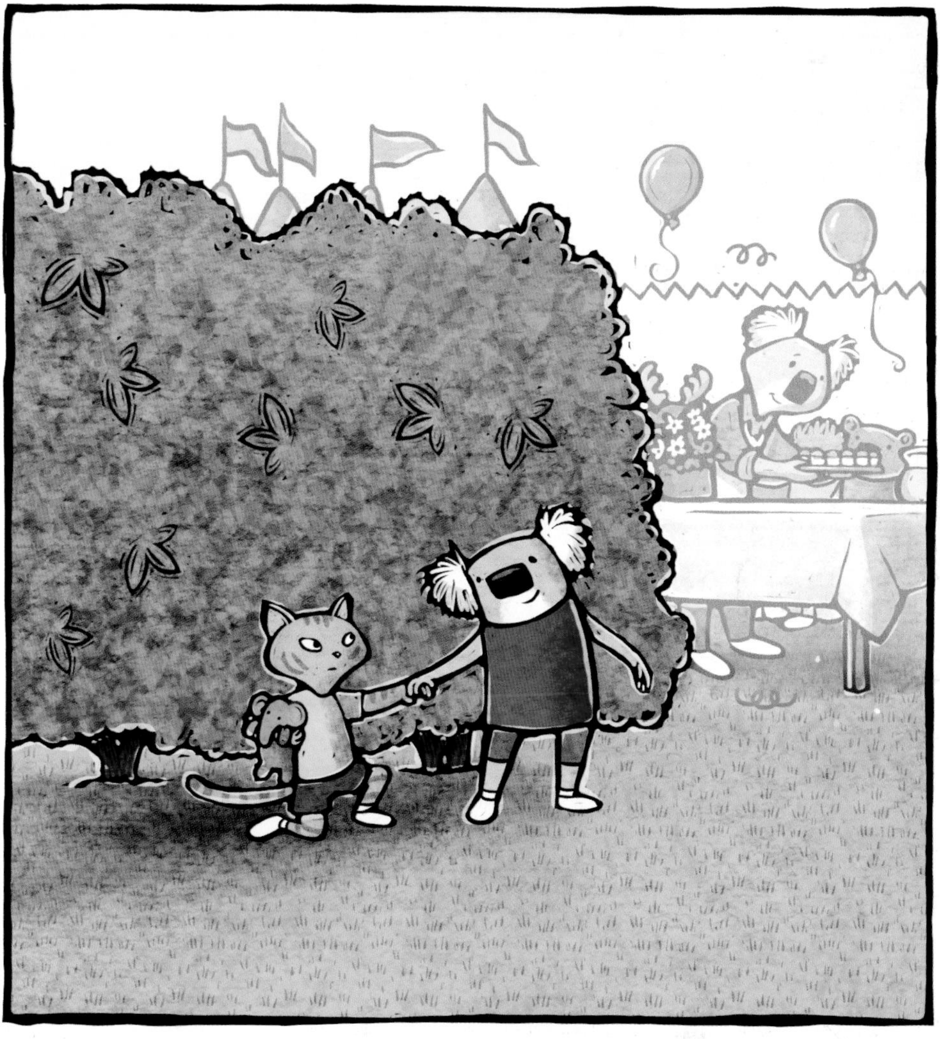

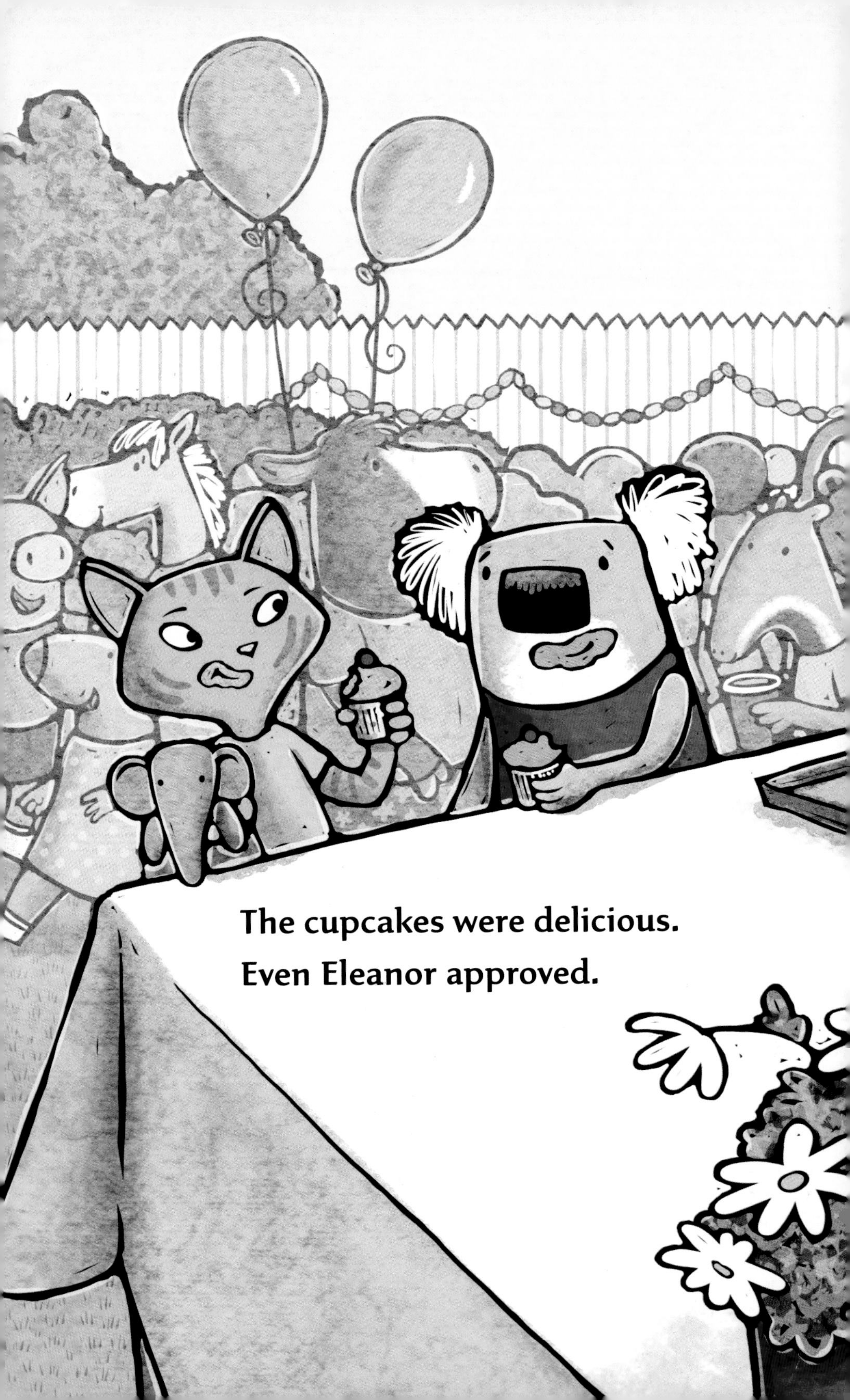

The cupcakes were delicious.
Even Eleanor approved.

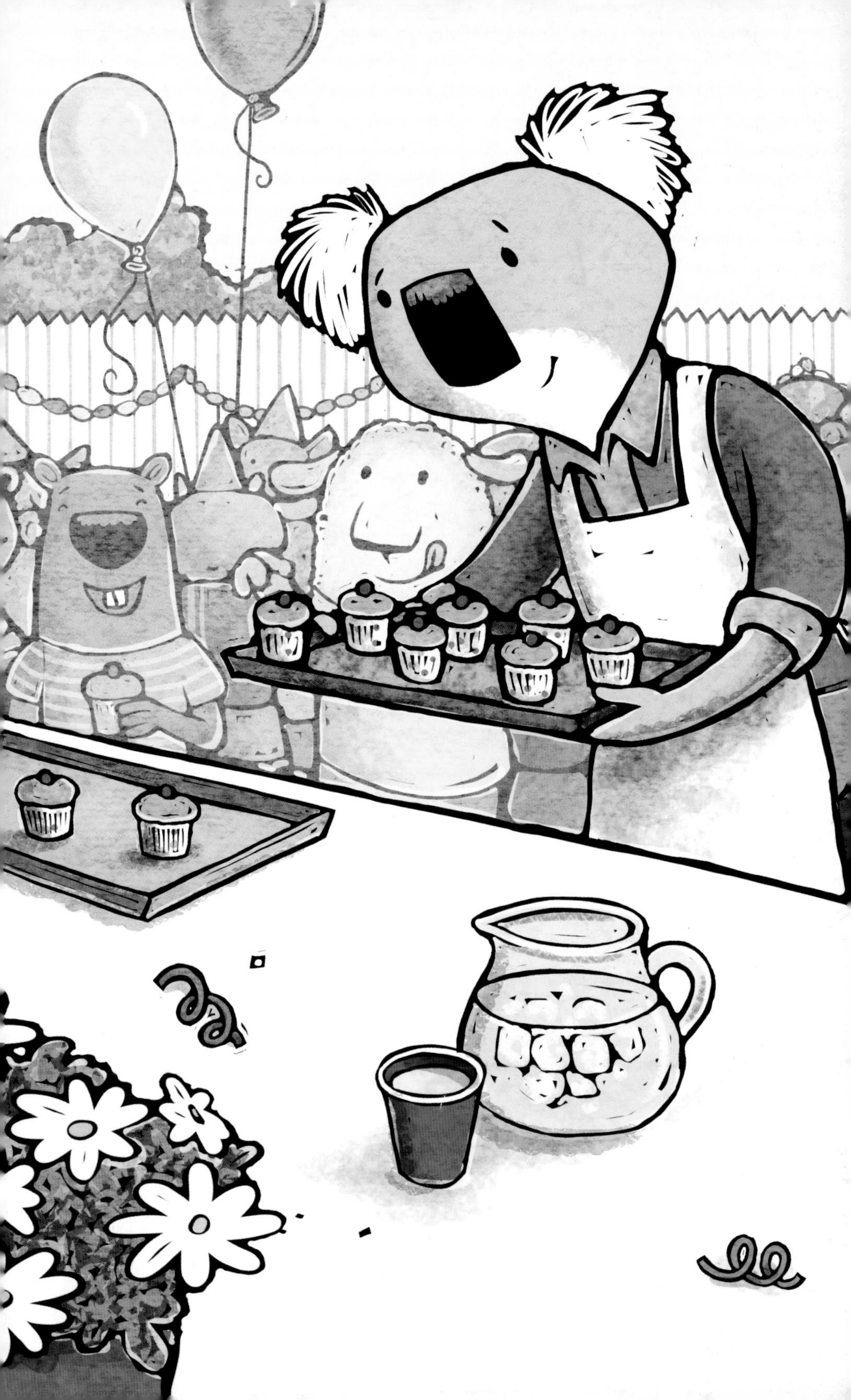

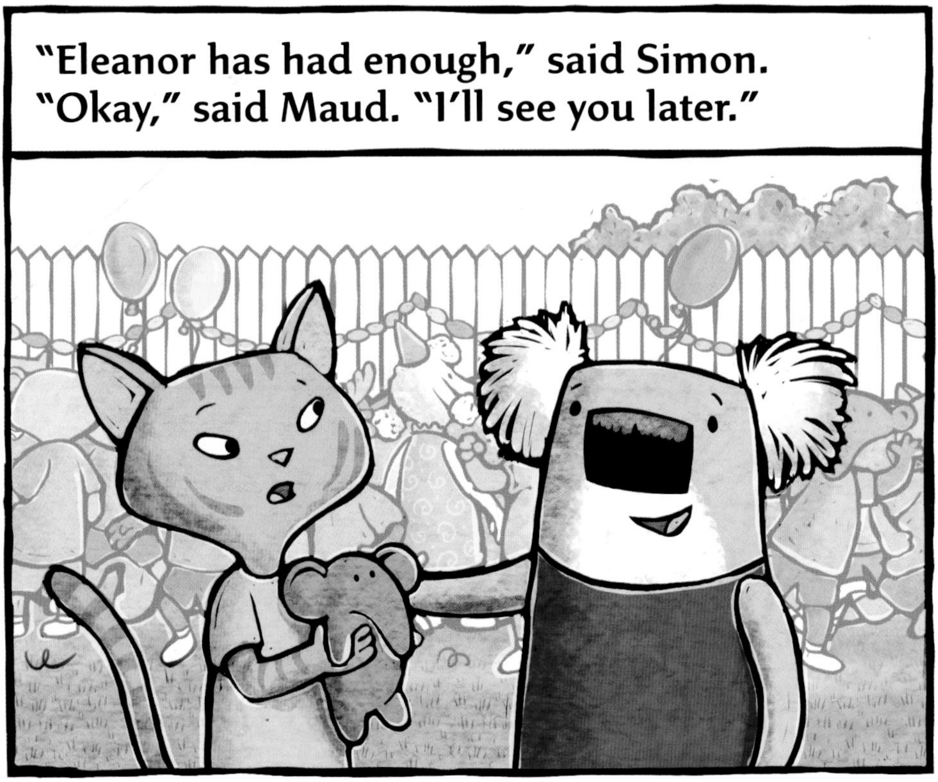
"Eleanor has had enough," said Simon.
"Okay," said Maud. "I'll see you later."

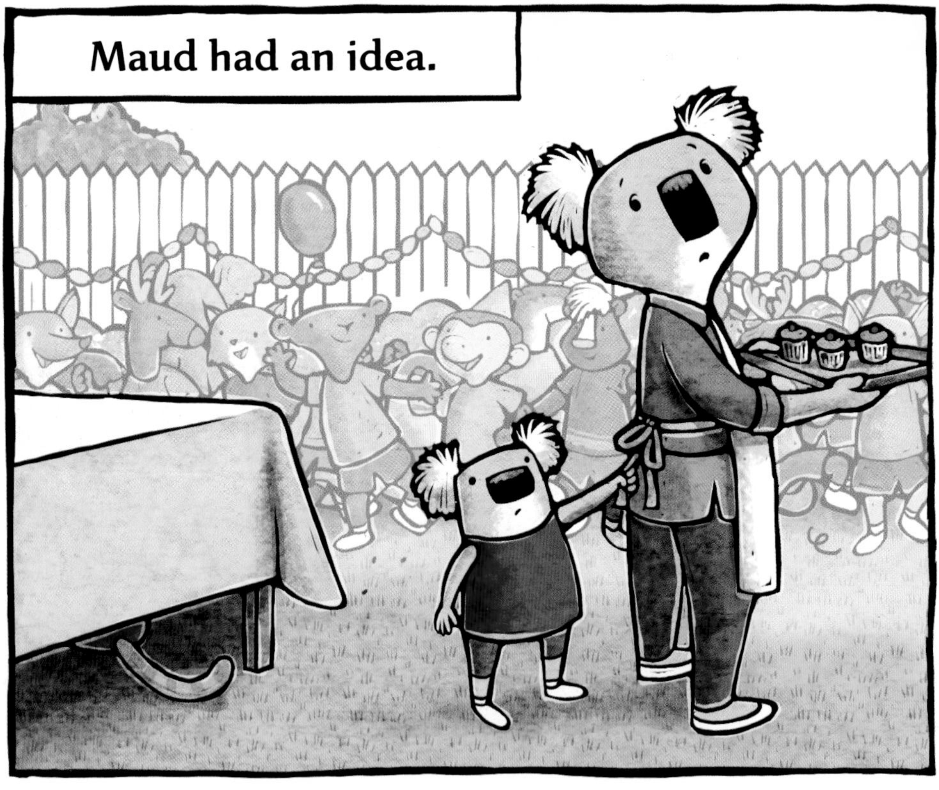
Maud had an idea.

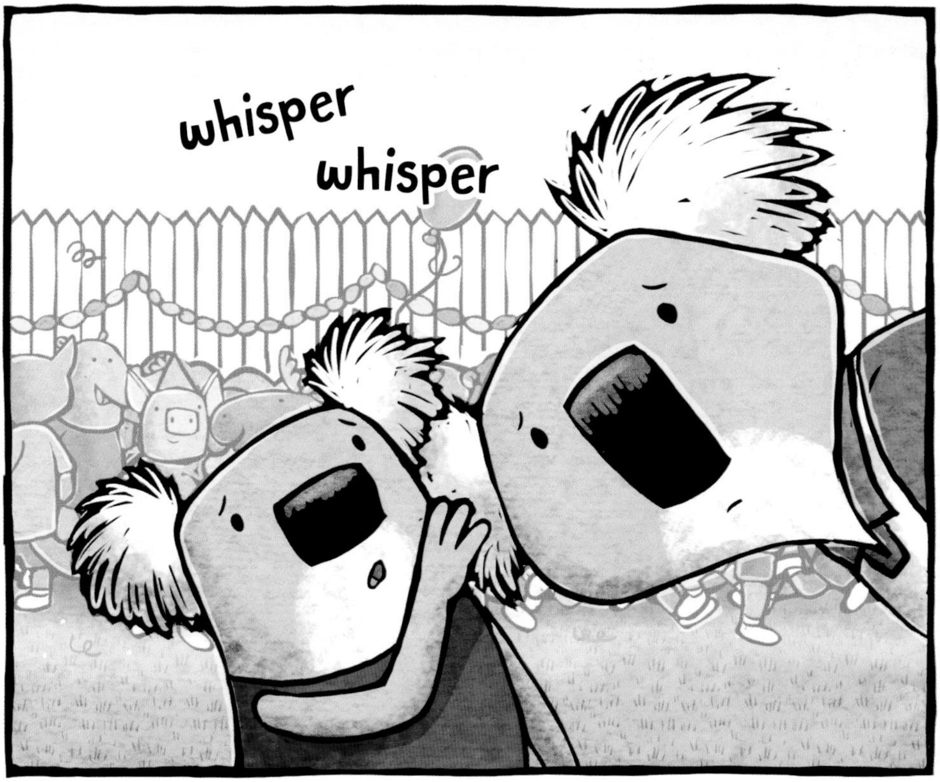
whisper
whisper

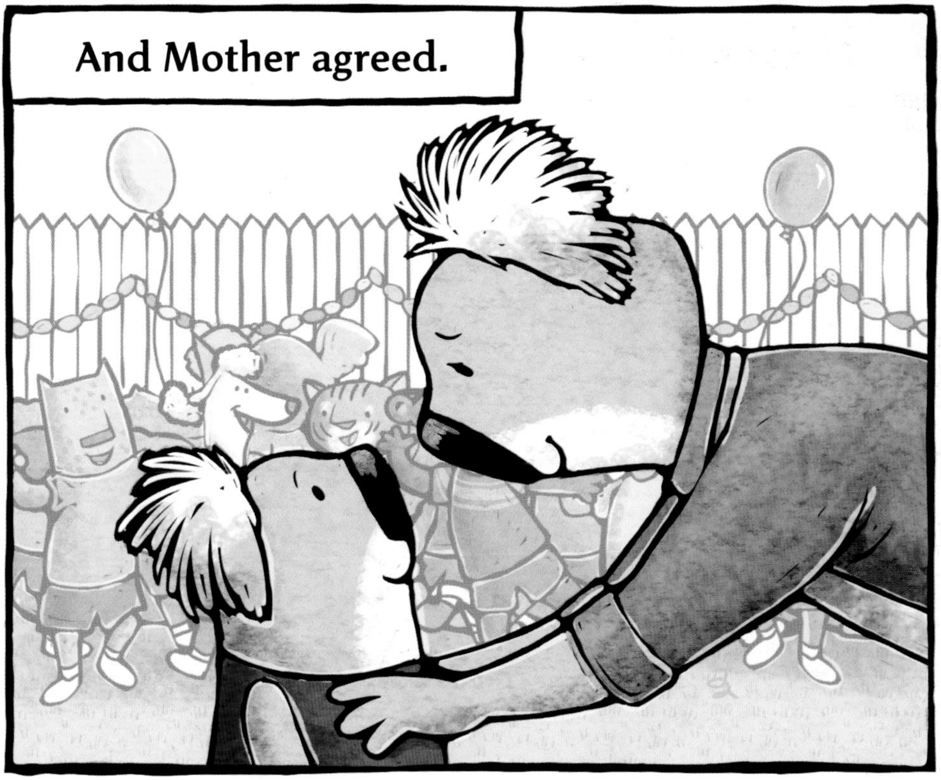
And Mother agreed.

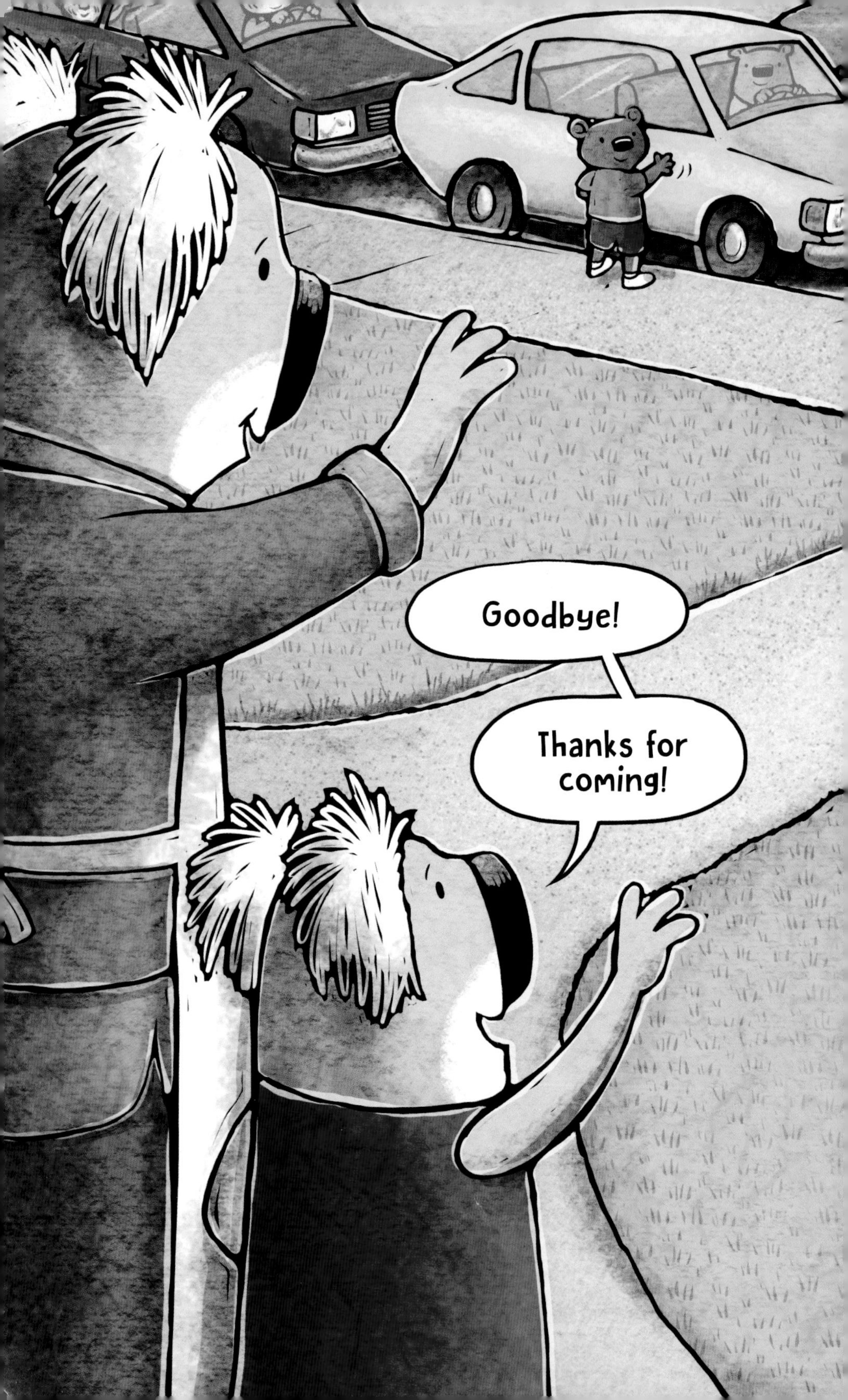
Goodbye!
Thanks for coming!

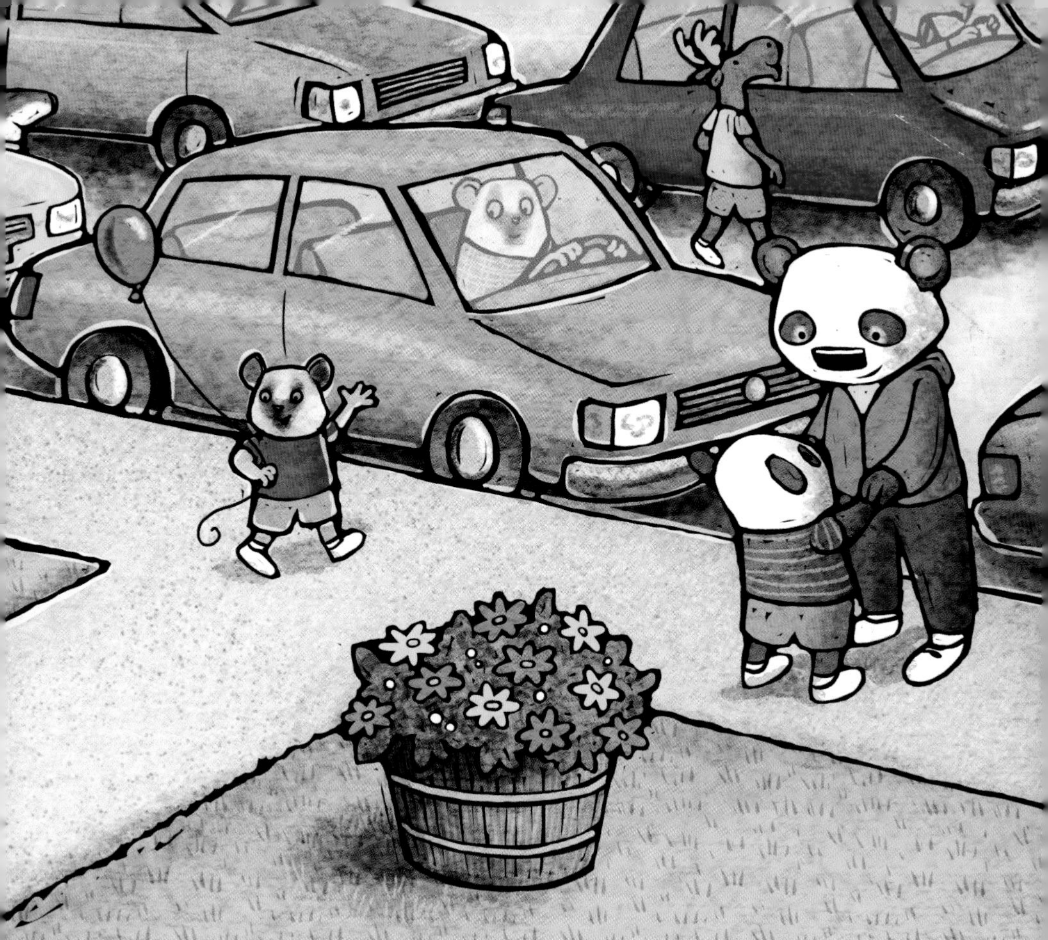

Later that afternoon, after all the other guests had gone . . .

Maud, Simon, and Eleanor had
a tiny little birthday party.

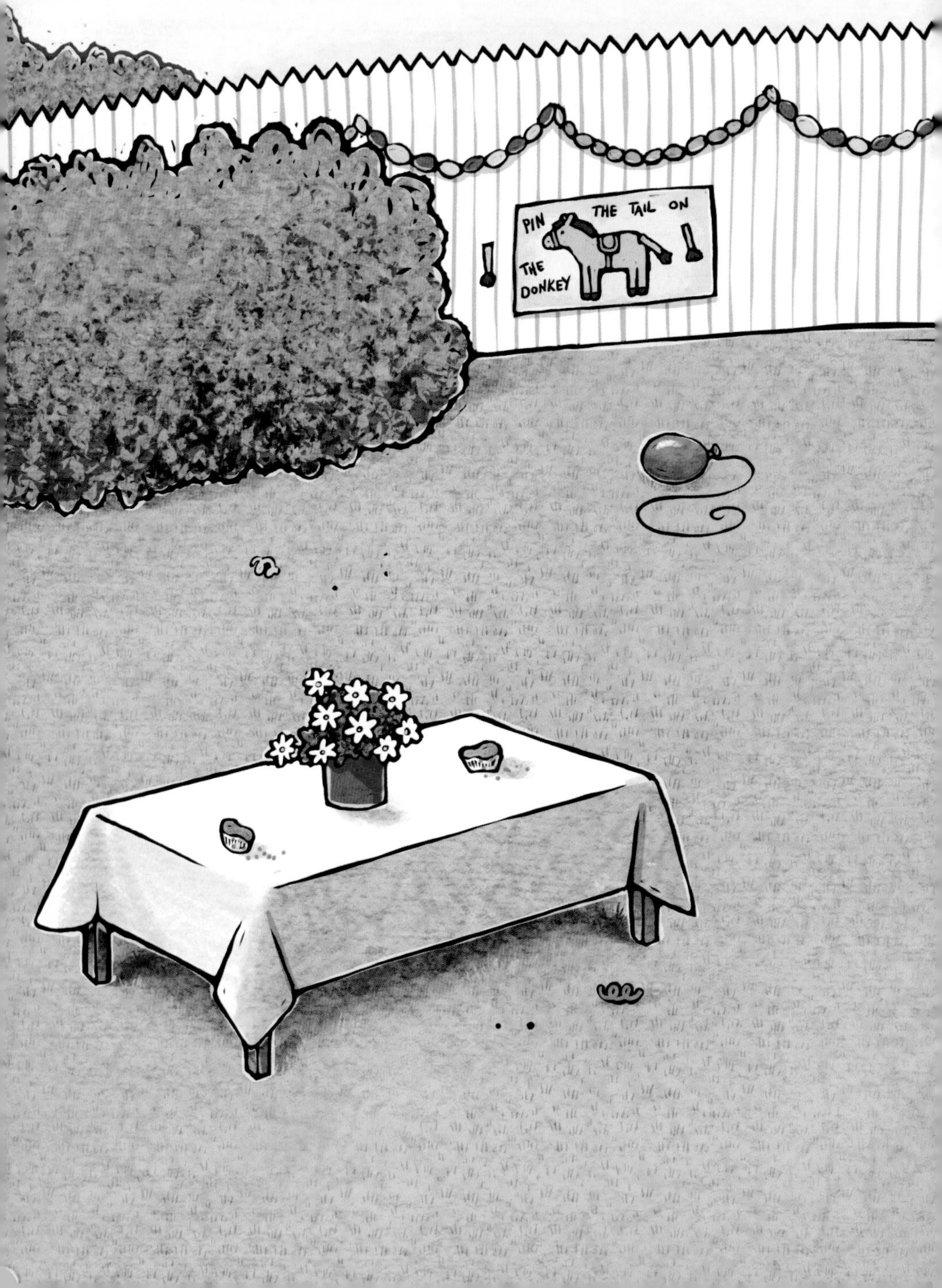
PIN THE TAIL ON THE DONKEY

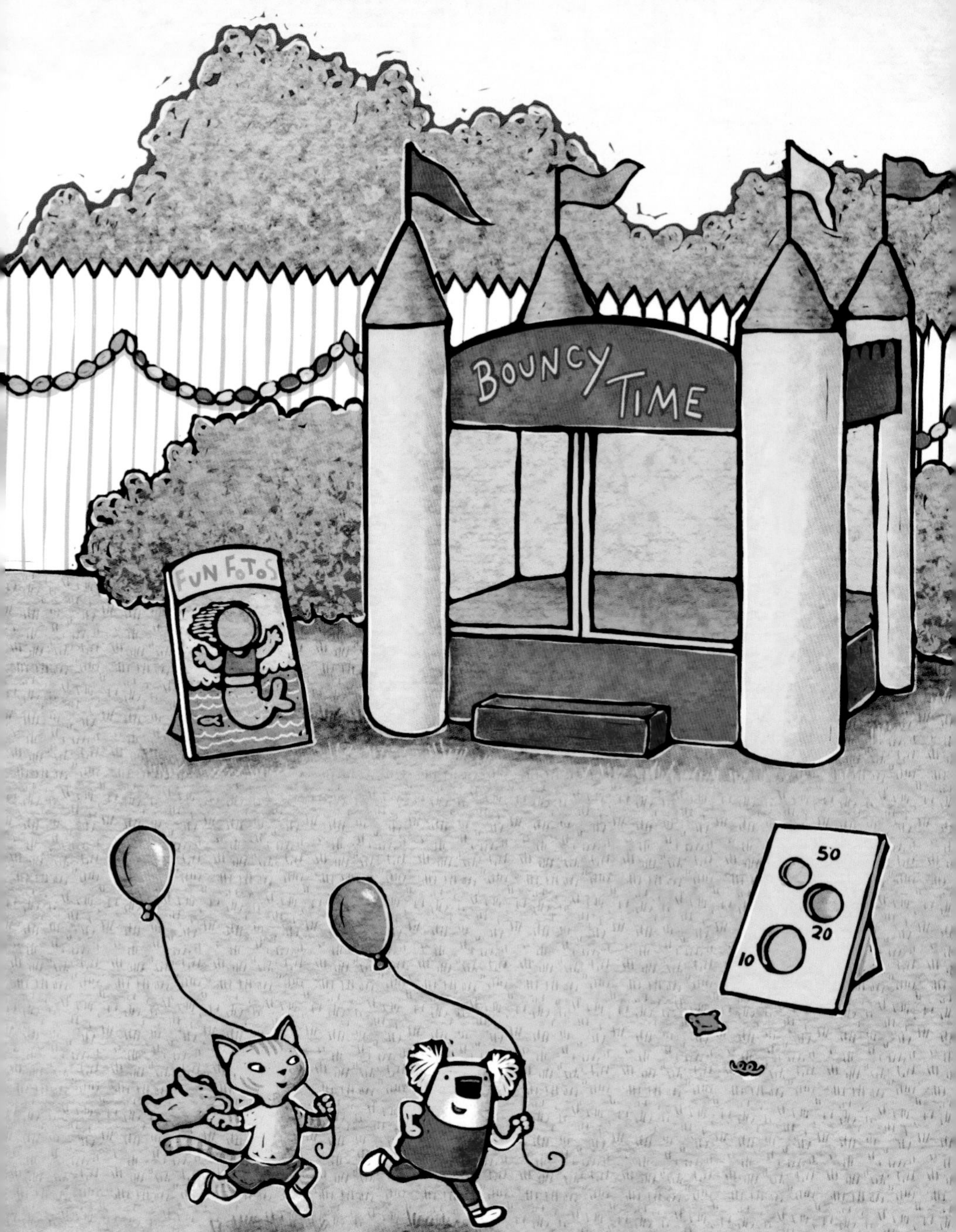
BOUNCY TIME
FUN FOTOS
50
20
10

And it was the best!

Note to Caregivers

Birthday parties are exciting events for children. As parents and caregivers, we want to make our child's special day a happy and memorable one. But some children aren't ready for huge celebrations. Some children, especially the very young and those with sensory sensitivities, can find parties overwhelming. It can be even more daunting when they are expected to be the center of attention.

Know your child and plan accordingly. Some children, like Maud, think they want a huge party but may not understand what that actually entails. Talk with your child before their big day and find a plan that makes everyone happy.

If children do find themselves in an overwhelming social situation, finding a quiet spot to take a break from the commotion can help alleviate their anxiety. Gently encouraging them to participate for small periods of time can help desensitize them to situations they find uncomfortable.